AIR ARIZONA

A Novel By

TOM SMITH

ISBN 1-890183-02-4

Wind Sock Press *
Post Office Box 55346
Phoenix, Arizona 85078-5346

* An imprint of the Compass Rose Publishing Group

This is a work of fiction. The characters, incidents and dialogues are products of the author's imagination, and are not to be construed as real. Where names of actual locations, establishments, military bases, aircraft squadrons and naval ships are used, the situations, incidents and activities are not intended to depict actual events or change the entirely fictional character of the work.

First printing, September 1997

Cover photo courtesy of Raytheon Aircraft Company

For my sometimes loony but always loving family—Jimmie, Launi, Stacy, Kelly, Becky, Travis, John, Stephanie, Shane and Rand. You never take me seriously. Please don't this time either!

And for Bonnie McAnerny, who took time out of her busy schedule to proof-read the manuscript and make suggestions.

CHAPTER 1

It was an ugly hulk—red and white at one time, but the colors had merged over the years sitting dormant in the desert, and the aircraft was now a sickly pink.

"What the hell is it?" Mike Murphy asked.

"What do you mean, what is it? It's a twin-Beech. You know...a C-45," answered Thaddeus Little.

"It doesn't look like a C-45 to me. Looks like a pile of shit. Where's the nose? The other engine? Most C-45's I've seen have two vertical stabilizers. That thing doesn't have any."

"Yeah, I know," Tad said. "That's why I got it so cheap. Twenty-five hundred."

"Twenty-five hundred? Where'd you get twenty-five hundred? Last week you didn't have twenty-five dollars. Who sold it to you...Ahab the Arab?"

"I sold the pickup...the Ford. Got three thousand for it. Got the plane at Litchfield Park across the road, Mike. The navy storage yard. They auctioned off some of their inventory."

"They auctioned off all their crap. That's what they did. That Beech was probably the biggest pile they had. What are you gonna do with it?" Mike took a Camel cigarette from his shirt pocket and lit up.

"Careful, Mike. The tanks are full of high octane fuel. They leave the tanks full, you know. Gas alone is worth a couple hundred bucks."

1

"Yeah, I can see the stains on the wings where the fuel's been leaking. Best thing I could do for you is blow the damn thing up." Mike Murphy threw the cigarette to the ground, squashing it with the toe of his boot.

"We've been talking for months, Mike. Getting a plane and starting a flying service. Well, now we've got one." Tad stepped on the cigarette to insure it was out.

"That`s not an airplane. It's a piece of junk. It`ll take another ten thousand...maybe more, to get it flying. I haven't got ten thousand ...have you?"

"Not now, Mike, but we can get it. We can sell some things. Borrow a few thousand. This is all we've talked about since you've been back."

"It`s all you've talked about, Tad. I'm still waiting to hear from United Airlines."

"United's not gonna hire you, Mike. You know that. American didn't want you. Even Bonanza turned you down. You don't spread an F-9 Cougar across the California desert showing off and get a job with the airlines. Hell, you didn't even make JG. Probably the only ensign in the navy that didn't make lieutenant junior grade. What the hell were you trying to do?"

"A little low level training...authorized low level training. We were supposed to fly low. I would have been okay if two blondes in a convertible hadn't waved. I made another low pass, and the chick in the right seat mooned me. I swear. They were on highway 60 just west of Blythe. I came back for a third pass to give them a real thrill. I went to full power, and a second later hit a sand dune. Never saw the damned thing. I wasn't more than thirty or forty feet above the ground."

"I don't know why you didn't kill yourself. From what I read in the papers, pieces of jet were scattered over several miles."

"Yeah. It really came unglued. It started coming apart when I bounced off the top of the dune. I was able to eject before it came back down. My chute barely opened before I hit the sand. The girls didn't even stop. They kept driving toward Blythe...still waving."

"You sure blew a good career, Mike. It's all you wanted to be since we were kids. Remember the movie, *High Barbaree*...and the *Men of the Fighting Lady*? We'd play and you`d always be the navy pilot, and I'd always be your gunner or engine mechanic."

"I remember. Someday I was gonna be an admiral."

"You were tops in your class outa flight training. But you always were a show-off...even in high school. You damn near cost us a win in the Tucson game when you ran outa bounds into the cheerleaders. I knew damn well you could have cut back and scored a touchdown. It's always women with you, isn't it? Get you in sniffing distance of a female and out the window goes logic."

"Don't give me a lecture, good buddy. Your military career didn't get too far either. You got tossed outa the air force before you completed four years. How many times did you go through detox ...three...four times?" Mike put another Camel in his mouth but didn't light it.

"I quit counting after the second time. It wasn't all my fault, you know? They stuck me up there in goddamned South Dakota. Wasn't anything to do up there but work...and drink. It was so damned cold on the line working on aircraft it took a pint or two just to get my blood flowing again. And the women...they weren't looking for a good time. They were looking for husbands. I didn't want any of that shit."

Michael Mitchell Murphy and Thaddeus Avery Little had grown up together in Phoenix, Arizona. What they had in common did not extend to their outward appearance. Mike Murphy was tall, six feet and a couple of inches. He had dark hair which curled in ringlets with moisture, thin lips, a square jaw with the constant hint of a five o'clock shadow, broad shoulders which tapered to a slim waist and hips. It could be reasonably said, Mike Murphy was handsome.

Tad Little was different, not only from Mike but from most other men. He was two inches shy of six feet in height. His hair was dirty dishwater in color and closely cropped. His face was a freckled full-moon which didn't see a razor until he joined the air force. His weight was deceptive, concentrated in his lower body. Most would guess his weight thirty to forty pounds lighter than it was. For all his awkward appearance, he was highly coordinated and understood all things mechanical.

Tad had been raised by his parents, his father an automobile mechanic and his mother a housewife. Two younger sisters had inherited the attractive looks of their mother, and both were popular in school. Tad inherited the round-face and beefy lower body of his father, and other than in sports, he enjoyed little popularity in school.

Mike's parents died in an automobile accident when he was five years of age. He was raised by an elderly aunt who furnished food and lodging, but little else. Mike had no other living relations.

Tad was a year ahead of Mike at the Garfield Elementary School until Tad failed the sixth grade. After that they were in the same class at the Emerson School for the seventh and eighth grades, and together at Phoenix Union High School where they graduated in 1949.

Both played football in high school, and basketball. Mike Murphy was an outstanding halfback and made the Arizona All State Team his senior year. Tad was a more than adequate football player at the guard position lettering both his junior and senior years. Neither was a good basketball player, but both made the team though they did not always travel to away games. Mike suspected the coach kept them on the basketball team to keep them in shape for the football season. Together they shared a number of interests. Other than Doris Dushane, who taught them both the joy and pleasure of carnal activities, these interests included automobiles—they were always rebuilding old cars; auto racing—Tad built a jalopy which Mike, lying about his age, drove several times at the South Mountain Speedway before totaling it in a spectacular end-over-end crash; and airplanes—both had joined the Civil Air Patrol at Sky Harbor Airport their sophomore year and had flights in a J-3 Piper Cub and Stearman bi-plane.

Following graduation from high school, Mike entered Arizona

AIR ARIZONA

State University on a football scholarship, and Tad went to work for a Plymouth-Dodge dealership in Phoenix as an apprentice mechanic.

Mike's football career ended, and also his scholarship, at the beginning of his sophomore year when he severely twisted his knee in practice. He considered dropping out of college and enlisting in the navy, but the navy recruiter informed him that if he completed four years of college, he could enter the navy as an officer and even go to flight training if he desired. He dropped the arduous engineering curriculum he had selected and switched to the easier political science major.

After a year at the Plymouth-Dodge dealership, a year of doing all the dirty little jobs in an automobile repair shop, Tad Little and Mike Murphy loaded up on a dozen beef tacos and four pitchers of beer at the Tepee Mexican Restaurant on East Indian School Road. The next morning a hung-over Tad Little departed Sky Harbor Airport for San Antonio, Texas, and the U. S. Air Force. Mike Murphy, also battling a head-busting hang-over, saw him off.

Mike Murphy continued his schooling at Arizona State University, using grants and government loans, and working five nights a week bussing tables in a nearby restaurant. In the early spring of 1953, he applied for U. S. Navy Officer Candidate School and was accepted contingent upon his graduation in May. He reported to OCS at Newport, Rhode Island in August, and after a whirlwind of study and military drill, reported to the naval air station, Pensacola, Florida, in early November as an Ensign, U. S. Naval Reserve, to commence flight training.

During these years Mike Murphy and Tad Little grew apart, neither being the type to correspond, and their leave periods never coincided.

In February of 1956, Ensign Michael Murphy completed his two years of obligated service after receiving his wings and was released from active duty. Poor performance reports based on his accident prevented him from remaining on active duty. He applied for pilot positions with a number of airlines but none responded. Back in Phoenix, a quick stop by the Tepee for a few beers and tacos in mid-March linked six long years. At the other end of the bar, working on his fourth, fifth or sixth Tequila, sat Thaddeus Avery Little.

"Come on, Mike, we can make this thing work. I know we can." Tad Little took a crumpled piece of paper from his shirt pocket. "Here's a list of what we need." Tad spread the paper out on the port wing near the fuselage of the C-45.

"Looks like a damn short list to me," Mike said, shaking his head. "You're gonna need a lot more paper than that to write down all we need."

"I know. So far I have one engine. I figure we can get an old one and rebuild it. I have my A and E license. Got that before I got out of the air force. We`ll need two vertical fin stabilizers and a nose cone, probably some brakes and tires, paint...maybe some radio gear. I haven't checked that yet." Tad checked off the items on his list.

"Let me add a few things to that, good buddy. Those fuel cells will have to be resealed. They're leaking like sieves. If I`m not mistaken, there's a kit you have to install to convert the military model to civilian use. The radios are probably wasted. I haven`t even looked at the interior, but from what I've seen on the outside, I imagine there's some expensive refurbishing to do in there."

"I know, Mike. There are probably several other things, too. But we won`t know if we don`t try. We'll be in the hole for awhile but I know we can make it. Please, Mike."

"Another thing," Mike added, "if I'm gonna fly it, I'll need a multi-engine rating. I've got my single-engine and instrument ratings...got those in the navy. I'll need at least ten hours in multi-engine and an FAA check ride. That's not cheap. I've never flown anything with more than one engine...and most of what I have is jet."

"Jesus, Mike. I didn't know it was all that complicated." Tad jotted down a few more notes on the sheet of paper. A broad smile crept across his round face. "Say, aren't you still in the reserves?"

"Inactive. They wouldn't let me continue on active duty." Mike fished through his shirt pockets for another cigarette.

"Couldn't you join the weekend warriors and get checked out in a C-45?"

"Maybe. They've been bugging me to join a reserve outfit. There's a reserve field at Los Alamitos, near Los Angeles. Don't know what kind of squadrons they have there, but I'm sure the air station has a C-45. Most do. Maybe I could finagle my way into it."

"See, Mike. I told you we could do it. We just have to cut a few corners." Tad Little beamed.

"Wait a minute! We haven't even mentioned money, Tad. You know, the green stuff that makes things like this happen."

"I think I might have some of that solved. How much do you think we'll need, Mike? Honestly."

"Bottom line...I'd say about thirty thousand. Got that much solved?"

"Mike, you remember Doris Dushane? Phoenix Union High School."

"*Drop-her drawers-Doris?* She probably screwed half the male population at the school. Sure taught me a few things, and you too, as I recall."

"I saw her last week, Mike. I took a short-cut through Goldwaters to get to the mall. She was at the cosmetic counter."

"Good job for Doris. Probably meets a lot of men buying perfume for their wives and girlfriends." Mike started to light the cigarette in his mouth but remembered the leaking fuel cells.

"She wasn't selling. She was buying. A lot of fancy expensive stuff. She recognized me and offered to buy me a drink. We went to that little bar at the south end of the mall."

"Did she proposition you, Tad?"

"No. She asked about you, Mike. I told her you were back in town. She wants to see you."

"Great! I could handle a little more of that, but how is that gonna get us thirty thousand dollars?"

AIR ARIZONA

"She's screwed a lot of guys, Mike. No doubt about it. But one of those guys was J. Preston Kissling, President of the Copper State Bank. She screwed him on their honeymoon, and old J. Preston dropped dead on a down stroke. *Drop-her-drawers-Doris* now lives in Paradise Valley and is worth several million bucks...at least. Mike, she wants to see you. I think she still has the hots for you."

CHAPTER 2

Mike Murphy stopped at the curb, dropping the butt of his cigarette into the gutter and smashing it with his freshly polished right shoe. He straightened his tie and tugged at the bottom of his navy blue blazer to remove the wrinkles. Finally he took a container from his gray trousers pocket and sprayed a fine mist of Binaca into his mouth, three sprays.

He walked North on Central Avenue for a half block and into the entrance door of Durant's Restaurant. He was nervous.

The *maitre-de* greeted him. "You have a reservation, sir?"

"Yes, Mike Murphy. Party of two. I called earlier."

"Oh yes, Mr. Murphy. Party of two. Welcome to Durant's."

"A lady friend will join me shortly," Mike said.

"Right this way, Mr. Murphy. First time at Durant's?"

Mike straightened his tie again. "Yes, first time." He followed the tall man in a dark suit to a table near the back of the elegant restaurant. The patrons, mostly middle-aged men dressed in business suits, talked with their hands, some using pens to write information on small note pads. It was definitely a businessman's restaurant. Big business.

"Your waiter will be here just as soon as your friend joins you. Care for a drink sir? I'll send a girl right over."

Mike sat in a chair that allowed him to see the entrance. He took a nervous drink of water and waited for Doris Dushane Kissling to arrive.

The wait was short. She entered the door brushing by the *maitre-de* and made a beeline to the back table. She was tall, five foot seven or eight, dressed in a well-tailored powder blue suit which accentuated her statuesque body. Her red hair was swept up in a French twist.

"Mike, so good to see you." She extended her left hand. Mike Murphy stood and accepted the hand she offered, noting the large diamond ring on her third finger. She turned her left cheek to Mike and he placed an awkward kiss on it. They both sat.

"It`s been a long time, Doris. Seven years?"

"More like eight, Mike. You're looking great. The navy must have been good for you." Her limpid green eyes stared directly into his.

"You too, Doris. You look...ah...real good." Mike took another drink of water and cleared his throat.

The *maitre-de* approached the table rapidly. "Mrs. Kissling, how good to see you. I didn't know you were dining with us today. I'm so sorry. I would have had a nice table up front for you. I can move you now, if you like."

Doris flashed a broad smile. "Thanks, Joe. This table is fine. I'm having lunch with an old friend."

An attractive young lady dressed in a short black skirt and low-cut white blouse came to the table. "Cocktails?"

"Hmmm, sounds good," Doris crooned. "What would you like, Mike? My treat, you know. I won't have it any other way."

"A beer, I guess. Budweiser."

"I'll have a Manhattan on the rocks, please. Three cherries," Doris said to the cocktail waitress.

"Wait a minute. Changed my mind," Mike interjected. "Bring me a gin martini on the rocks. Beefeaters. Three olives."

Doris Kissling smiled. "Good, Mike. A martini will loosen you up. You look a little up-tight to me."

"I guess I am, Doris. I didn't know what to expect. Tad said you lost your husband. Was that recently?"

"About a year ago. I've been pretty busy since. Keeps my mind off his passing. He was a wonderful man, J. P. He made sure I had everything I wanted. Older men are so much more understanding." Doris adjusted the large ring on her finger.

Mike took a Camel cigarette from his coat pocket. "Cigarette, Doris?"

"Thanks, Mike, but I don't smoke."

"I'm sorry." Mike started to return the cigarette to its package.

"You can smoke, Mike. I don't mind. J. P. smoked. Cigars mostly."

The waiter, a middle-aged man in a dark suit, came to the table. "Mrs. Kissling, how good to see you. What may I serve you today?"

"My usual, George. Spinach salad."

"And you, sir. I recommend our prime rib today. It is excellent."

"I`m sure it is," Mike responded. "Just bring me what Mrs. Kissling is having."

"Are you sure, Mike?" Doris placed her left hand on Mike's right hand. "You`re a big healthy hunk of a man. You should eat more than just a salad."

"The salad's fine. I've put on a little weight since I got outa the navy."

"Looks good on you, Mike. Tell me about the navy. Tad said you were a pilot. Jets, I believe he said. Sounds exciting."

"It was. I was in a carrier based fighter squadron. Flew the F-9 Cougar. A great airplane. I got in just at the tail end of the Korean thing."

"I always knew you were the hero-type, Mike. I had quite a crush on you in high school, you know?" She leaned over the table toward Mike.

"We did have some pretty good times, Doris." Mike crushed out his cigarette in the ash tray and wiped his mouth with a napkin. "What do you have planned for this afternoon? Maybe we could catch up on old times."

"You mean go somewhere together? My place...or yours? Maybe a motel. Gee, we could slip off our clothes, climb in the sack and pick up right where we left off...eight years ago."

"Sounds great to me, Doris. I don't have anything else planned for the day."

"Screw you, Mike Murphy! I didn't come here to get laid. I can get that anytime I want from guys a whole lot better at it than you. I came here for business. Tad said you had a business deal for me. Something about airplanes and a flying service. I don't know crap about airplanes, or flying services, but I do know crap about money and how to invest it."

The drinks arrived at the table. Doris raised her glass to Mike. "Cheers," she said with a smile.

"Cheers, Mrs. Kissling." Mike downed the martini in a single gulp. "Miss," he said to the cocktail waitress. "Another martini, please. A double. Forget the olives."

CHAPTER 3

Mike Murphy eased his MG roadster into the covered parking space designated for the apartment he and Tad Little shared. A light in the window of the apartment complex on East Indian School Road told Mike that his friend was still awake. It was after midnight. Mike climbed the stairs hesitantly to the second level. He balanced himself with the handrail, pausing frequently. Finally he reached apartment number 2110 and tried to insert the key into the lock, a more difficult task this evening than usual.

The door opened inward without the key inserted.

"Jesus Christ, Mike! Where you been?" Tad Little stood in the open doorway dressed in cut-off jeans and a grease-stained T-shirt. "Shit, Mike! You're so drunk you can't stand up. You been shacked up with Doris?"

"Shacked up? With Doris?" Mike stumbled through the door dropping to a nearby couch. "I don't think so."

"Lunch was at one, Mike. One o'clock. It's after midnight now. How long can you screw?"

"Not sure. Never tried for a record. Probably several days, I guess. How about you, Tad. How long can you screw?"

"Goddamnit, Mike, what happened? Did you get some money? How'd you get so loaded?" Tad helped Mike remove his shoes, a task that Mike was experiencing some difficulty in accomplishing. "Let me make you some coffee, then tell me what the hell happened."

13

Tad went to the small kitchen and put a pan of water on the gas burner. Mike Murphy, with much difficulty, removed his socks, shirt and trousers. He sat there in his Fruit-of-the-Loom briefs and stared at the ceiling. "Air Arizona," he said aloud. "Silver and turquoise." Tad returned with a steaming cup of instant coffee. He handed the cup to Mike. "What'd you say, Mike? I didn't understand what you said."

Mike didn't answer. He took several gulps of the black liquid then shook his head. "Damn! That's hot." He placed the cup on the nearby table. "Quite a lady, Doris Dushane Kissling. Quite a lady."

"Come on, Mike. Tell me what happened. Did you get some money? She said she was willing to help." Tad handed the cup back to Mike. "Here, drink this."

Mike took several more sips. "What the hell did you tell her, Tad? She knew a lot more than I did about everything."

"I told her you were back in town...outa the navy. That we wanted to start a flying service...do some charter work...and stuff. We were looking for a small loan. Maybe a partner."

"Partner? You didn't say a damn thing to me about a partner. I thought you wanted me to have lunch with her. Lay on a little charm. Jump in the sack for an hour or two and then hit her up for five or ten thousand."

"That's right, Mike. That's all I wanted. Did you get some dough?" Tad took the empty cup from Mike's hand. "Let me get you another cup."

A quick trip to the kitchen provided a second cup of strong black coffee. "Drink this, Mike."

"Okay, I'm doing better. Goddamned gin about ripped my head off."

"What'd you two do...drink all afternoon and night?"

"Not us two. Our meeting lasted all of thirty minutes. She told the bartender to take care of me after she left and to put it on her tab. You had better sit down, good buddy. I've got some real shit to put on you." Mike reached into his trouser pocket and removed a small wad of crumpled paper. "See if I can read all of this."

"Money, Mike. Did you get some money?"

"You bet your sweet ass we got money...and a lot more. For starters, she's willing to front two hundred thousand dollars. More if we need it."

"Two hundred thousand?" Tad leapt to his feet. "That's great!"

"Sit down, Tad. There's a few strings attached. More like ropes." Mike smoothed out the wadded sheet of paper. "We'll be incorporated as Air Arizona. Mrs. Doris Dushane Kissling will be the president of the corporation and own seventy-five percent of the operation. You'll be the director of maintenance and I'll be the director of operations. We'll each own twelve and a half percent of the company. The aircraft, and all future aircraft, will be painted silver with turquoise trim. We'll operate out of small Quonset hangar and office on Air Lane Boulevard at Sky Harbor Airport. You and I will run the company on a day-to-day basis, but she`ll have the final say on any major expenditures. We have to show a profit after one year. If not, we're dissolved. Now, did I leave anything out?" Mike turned the paper over and looked at the back side. "No. I think that's about it, Mr. Director of Maintenance."

"Jesus!" Tad let loose a low whistle.

"She had this shit already drawn up by her attorney," Mike said. "I couldn't believe it. She played me for a real idiot."

"Damn, Mike. I didn't know. I thought she just wanted to help us out. What do you think?"

"I think that *Drop-her-drawers-Doris* has grown a set of balls since we last slept with her."

CHAPTER 4

On March 4, 1957, the last remains of the Beechcraft Model C-45, designated 51086 by the Bureau of Naval Air, was unceremoniously loaded on a flatbed truck in a vacant field in Litchfield Park, Arizona, and driven to its new home at Sky Harbor Airport in Phoenix. To accomplish this, the wing was removed from the fuselage adding several more thousand dollars to the restoration project.

Immediately upon its arrival at Sky Harbor, Tad Little, assisted by a young Native-American with the honest-to-goodness name of Buck Skin, went to work putting the little twin-engine craft back together. Aircraft plans and maintenance manuals were scattered in various locations on the oil-stained concrete floor of the small hangar. On Saturday, March 9, while Tad Little and Buck Skin labored over the first and only airplane owned by Air Arizona, Michael M. Murphy, Ensign, U. S. Naval Reserve, reported to the commanding officer of Naval Air Station, Los Alamitos, California, for reserve duty. He was to report the second weekend of each month and for a two week period each summer to fulfill his reserve obligation. Normally, reserve aviators flew with the squadrons based at the air station, but given Ensign Murphy's reputation, squadron commanders were relieved that he requested assignment to the air station to fly the C-45.

Ensign Murphy`s first orientation flight in the Beechcraft, under the instruction of Naval Aviation Chief Petty Officer Paul Dumas, one of the few remaining enlisted navy pilots on active duty, resulted in two ground loops on taxi-out, a swerve into the grass beside the runway on takeoff and a four-bounce landing. That was Saturday. On Sunday the flight suffered from only one ground loop on taxi, a corrected swerve on takeoff and a two-bounce landing. Chief Dumas seemed unconcerned, his only comment being: "Goddamned jet pilots!"

An engine for Air Arizona One was delivered to Sky Harbor on the 13th of March, purchased through a catalog that Tad Little had ordered through the mail, and by midnight, was hung on the port wing of the C-45 by Tad and Buck. This major accomplishment was celebrated by the sharing of a quart bottle of tequila. Mike Murphy sat in a folding chair observing the maintenance work, consuming a six pack of Budweiser and seriously wondering if after all their hard work, he wouldn't tear the damn thing up trying to fly it.

By the end of March the two vertical stabilizers and a nose cone had been installed. Resealing the fuel cells was scheduled for the first week in April. Tires, brakes, a VHF transceiver, a VOR omni receiver, forty gallons of silver paint and two gallons of turquoise paint were on order.

On April 13 and 14, Ensign Mike Murphy received two more check-out flights in Los Alamitos' C-45 aircraft without a ground loop on taxi, or noticeable swerve on takeoff, and with only one-bounce landings. Chief Dumas signed off Mike's log book: *Qualified C-45*.

With ten hours flight time in the twin-Beech, Mike applied for his multi-engine endorsement on his FAA commercial pilot license. With his navy qualification, he was not required to take an FAA flight check.

Two months had passed since the incorporation of Air Arizona, and Doris Dushane Kissling had not set foot into the hangar or office on East Air Lane Boulevard. She had not called. She had not communicated. She had merely established a two hundred thousand dollar line of credit at the Copper State National Bank. Tad Little was depleting the line of credit rapidly.

In August, Ensign Murphy was promoted to Lieutenant JG, USNR and completed his two weeks active duty training at Los Alamitos. He flew the C-45 daily, sometimes twice, logging every hour possible in the formidable navy *bugsmasher*. He navigated airways, shot instrument approaches and landings, practiced emergency procedures. He now taxied without ground looping, swerved only marginally on takeoff, flew and landed with one engine simulated out and, in general, became about as competent as any aviator who ever got in the C-45 twin-Beechcraft, which had a nasty habit of jumping up and biting pilots just when they had it figured out.

On November 21, 1957, Air Arizona held an open house at the hangar on Air Lane Boulevard. The twin-Beech was splendid in its silver colored coat with turquoise trim and a turquoise symbol on each vertical stabilizer. Buck had painted the symbols which he said meant *spirit in the clouds*. All local newspapers had been notified of the open house and ceremony, although only the Paradise Valley Shopper's Guide attended, offering an article in their weekly shopper in exchange for a quarter-page advertisement.

The highlight of the open house, after the introduction of the director of operations and chief pilot (the only pilot!) Michael Murphy and the director of maintenance, Thaddeus Little, was the breaking of a bottle of vintage 1956 California champagne on the silver colored nose cone. The nose cone broke loose and fell to the hangar floor.

CHAPTER 5

November 22, 1957, the first full day of operation for Air Arizona and charter flight number one was already scheduled. Tad Little called Mike Murphy at 6:15 A.M. "Up and at'em, Mike. We`ve got a charter. Buck and I've been up all night reattaching the nose cone and insuring the log books are accurate and up to date. You know FAA has a nasty habit of popping in unexpectedly and digging through your records. Anyhow, about ten minutes ago I get a call from a guy in Gila Bend who wants us to be there by eight. Get a move on, Mike,"

At five minutes past seven, Mike scooted through the hangar door. Tad was removing the last of the passenger seats.

"What'd we have, Tad? Must be a cargo flight. I see you have all the seats out." Mike went into the small office.

Tad followed. "Sort of."

"I don't see anything written on the board." Mike looked at the large Plexiglas board on the office wall. It had columns for date, time, departure base, load and remarks.

"I didn't have time to put it on the board, Mike. The fuel truck's headed here now. I've got the bird all pre-flighted. We should be ready to go in about fifteen minutes or so."

"What's the load, Tad? I need to know."

"A bull. We have to—"

"A bull? Jesus Christ, are you kidding me? I'm not up to practical jokes this morning."

19

AIR ARIZONA

"It's just a baby bull, Mike. A small one. We have to have it in Las Vegas for a stock show by one this afternoon." Tad turned his head so as not to look directly at Mike Murphy.

"A goddamned bull will kick the Beech to pieces, Tad. Crap all over the deck. We can't haul a bull to Las Vegas." Mike poured a cup of hot coffee from a percolator on the desk.

"It'll be tranquilized, Mike. The man said he would be as docile as a lamb. He'll be tethered front and rear. Besides, one of his wranglers will ride along with it. A thousand bucks, Mike, if we can get it there by one o'clock."

"How much?" Mike pulled a cigarette from his shirt pocket.

"A thousand bucks. One thousand dollars. This ain't no ordinary bull, Mike. It's a national champion."

"How much does the damn thing weigh? Did you even ask?"

"No. How much can a baby bull weigh...a couple of hundred pounds? Not much more than me. It shouldn't be a problem weight-wise." Tad poured himself a cup of coffee. "Soon as the fuel`s onboard, we'll be ready to go."

Mike Murphy eased the twin-Beech onto the short 2800 foot runway at Gila Bend, Arizona. He brought the aircraft to a stop on the runway, unlocked the tailwheel, and with a burst of power on the starboard engine swung the craft around and taxied toward a large stake truck parked just off the runway. "That must be our cargo there." Mike pointed to the waiting truck.

Tad Little, seated in the copilot seat, nodded. "They said they would meet us here." It was 8:15 A.M. and a morning chill was in the air.

Mike taxied the plane off the runway stopping beside the truck. He pulled both mixture controls to off, and the props swung to a stop. He secured the magneto switches and snapped the battery switch to *Off*. Tad made his way to the rear of the cargo compartment.

A slim beanpole of a man stepped from the cab of the truck and waved. "A real slick looking áreoplane you got there, mister," the beanpole shouted to Tad Little as he exited the passenger door. "Ain't ever seen one painted up like that before."

Tad extended his hand to the cowpoke. "Tad Little, Air Arizona. You the man I talked to on the phone?"

"No'sir. Not me. That was Mr, Moore...the boss. He's already gone on to Vegas on one of them big jets outa Phoenix."

Mike stepped down from the rear door of the plane. "Bull in the truck? I want to take a look at him."

The beanpole pointed to the bed of the truck.

Mike stepped on the rear bumper and peered over the tailgate. "Shit! That ain`t no baby bull. Sonofabitch must weigh eight or nine hundred pounds. No way are we gonna get him through the door of the Beech."

The black animal sat on his haunches, his eyes pointing in different directions, his head flopping to and fro. Slobber dripped in long strings from his mouth.

"I gave him a double-shot," the beanpole said. "He won't be able to move for three or four hours. Mr. Moore will meet you at the airport in Vegas. Pay you there. That bull's his prize possession."

"Tad," Mike shouted from his perch on the rear of the truck. "Get over here and look at this sonofabitch. There's no way he'll fit through the door."

Tad climbed the rear bumper and stood beside Mike. "I'll get him in there, Mike. You just go have a cigarette and relax. I'll have him loaded in ten...fifteen minutes. A thousand bucks, Mike."

True to his word, Tad Little had the bull in the cargo compartment tethered head and rump to cargo hold-downs on the deck of the aircraft before 8:30.

Mike crushed out his cigarette and headed for the plane. "You going with us, mister?" he said to the beanpole cowboy.

"Not me," beanpole answered. "Mr. Garcia's going with you." He pointed to an older Hispanic man sitting in the right seat of the truck. "He don`t speak no English...and he won't understand much of what you say, but he's real good with that critter."

Mike walked to the door of the aircraft and inspected it. Black hair and bloody tissue stuck to the rim of the opening. "Goddamnit, Tad, what did you have to do to get him in there...chop off a few rib steaks?"

"He got stuck the first time we tried. His shoulders were too big. We greased him up and he slipped right in." Tad exhibited a broad smile knowing he had pulled off a near-to-impossible feat.

Mike signaled Mr. Garcia with a come-here gesture. The Mexican immediately fell to his knees, crossed himself, put his hands together and gazed skyward. He intoned a prayer in his native language. The only word Mike understood was *Dios* which the man used numerous times.

Mike looked at Tad. "What the hell is that all about?"

Tad shrugged his shoulders.

"Well, get his ass on board and let's get outa here." Mike entered the door and made his way by the tethered bull. The bull jerked his head. Snot flew from the bull's nose attaching itself to Mike's trousers. "Shit!" Mike shouted. The bull jerked again, emitting a large odorous volume of intestinal gas followed by a quart or more of brown liquid. Mike lurched forward to avoid the quivering animal and smartly put his right boot in the brown discharge.

The little Beechcraft skipped down the runway and vaulted into the blue Arizona sky. Mike raised the landing gear, set climb power on the throttles and turned to a northwesterly heading.

"What`s our flight time to Vegas, Mike?" Tad asked.

Mike Murphy did not answer. He stared straight ahead, his teeth clenched.

"Will we make it by...by one?" Tad was hesitant.

"Don't talk to me...goddamnit!"

"Come on, Mike. It's a thousand dollars."

"A thousand dollars...bullshit! It`ll cost more than that to clean up the airplane." Mike continued to stare straight ahead. "Is this what you had in mind when you said we'd start an air service? I sure as hell didn't. I pictured neat little packages...pouches of courier mail... hunting and fishing parties. I pictured sweet young things in short skirts or tight shorts. I sure didn't picture a snot-slinging, farting, crapping, wild-ass animal."

"I'm sorry, Mike. I just thought it would be, you know...an easy... ah, screw it!"

Mike leveled the twin Beech at 12,500 feet. He picked up the microphone and filed a visual flight plan with the Phoenix FAA radio.

They flew over Wickenburg, and nearly an hour later, over Kingman. The flight progressed smoothly. There was no commotion from the cargo compartment. Mr. Garcia sat on the deck coddling the bull's head in his lap. Mike began to relax.

"Sorry I got so pissed, Tad. I just couldn't believe we were doing this. We should be in Vegas in a little less than hour." Mike turned to Tad Little and smiled.

Tad nodded but did not speak. Lake Mead appeared on the horizon.

Mike eased back the throttles and started a gradual descent. "We'll start down now and cross Lake Mead at about five thousand."

As the small craft passed over the south shore of the lake, it began to pitch...nose high...nose low.

"Turbulence?" a concerned Tad Little asked.

Mike Murphy glanced over his right shoulder. "Turbulence. Hell no! That black sonofabitch is loose back there. Better get back there, Tad, before he kicks this bird apart, or causes us to stall and spin."

Suddenly the nose pitched down sharply. Mike reached for the trim wheel and rolled it full aft.

"Moooooo!" The bull thrust his head through the door into the cockpit. Slobber ran from his open mouth. Mucus flew from his wide nostrils.

"Get that sonofabitch back to the center of the cabin," Mike shouted to Tad Little. "Kill him if you have to. He's gonna put us right in the middle of Lake Mead."

Tad grabbed the snorting bull by the head forcing him back into the cargo compartment.

The pressure on the yoke eased. Mike brought the nose up to level flight at about 2000 feet above the lake's surface. He re-trimmed the aircraft for level flight. Looking back over his shoulder he could see Mr. Garcia restraining the animal. Tad was attempting to reattach the tethers .

Suddenly the nose pitch violently up. Mike saw that the bull had pinned the Mexican wrangler against the rear bulkhead of the cargo compartment. He pushed the yoke forward as hard as he could. Not enough! He rolled in full forward trim. The nose was a good 30 degrees above the horizon. The airspeed fell off rapidly. One hundred knots...ninety...eighty. The controls became sloppy, and Mike felt the shudder of an impending stall.

"Get up here, Tad," Mike screamed. "We're about to stall."

Tad clawed his way forward to the cockpit. With his weight forward, Mike was able to lower the nose. The airspeed stabilized. Tad climbed into the copilot seat and put additional forward force on the control yoke. The airspeed began a gradual increase.

"Jesus!" Mike said. "I thought we'd had it. What's going on back there now?"

"Mr. Garcia is giving him another shot. He should be out cold in a couple of minutes. I got the butt line reattached. He can`t move any further aft."

The nose dropped sharply again. The bull's rear entered the cockpit through the door. Bellowing loudly, he deposited a pile of excrement on the flight deck between the pilot seats.

"Here we go again...goddamnit!" Mike pulled the control yoke back as far as possible. "Get on the yoke with me, Tad. Pull as hard as you can. We're going right smack into the middle of the fuckin' lake."   "Mike...I'm scared...real scared,"

"You think I'm not," Mike shot back.

"Yeah...but you can swim. I can't."

"You silly sonofabitch! You're worried about swimming when the impact alone is gonna kill us."

CHAPTER 6

Mike Murphy sat in the cramped office of the Air Arizona hangar, his feet on the desk, a cup of black coffee on the typewriter shelf and the latest issue of *Playboy* magazine on his lap. Outside the office, in the maintenance space, Tad Little and Buck Skin labored diligently cleaning out Air Arizona One. Two days before, the aircraft had been badly soiled by the baby show bull they had delivered to Las Vegas. Only the last-minute heroics of the Hispanic wrangle, Mr. Garcia, had saved the craft from a watery grave and probably the lives of the three men onboard. He had managed to inject the raging animal with a tranquilizing drug and successfully returned him to the center of the cargo compartment. The phone on the desk jingled, arresting Mike's attention from the centerfold he was so carefully surveying. He accordioned the centerfold back into the magazine, dropped his feet to the floor, leaned forward and picked up the receiver. "Air Arizona operations, may I help you?"

"Good morning, Mike. I understand we've completed our first charter. Congratulations."

Mike immediately identified the voice on the phone. "Good morning, Mrs. Kissling."

"Come on, Mike. You can call me Doris. Business be damned, we're still good friends, I hope."

"Okay, Doris. How did you know about the charter?"

"Tad called me. Said we were paid a thousand dollars. Not bad.

How much of that was profit?"

"Don't know yet. We had a little damage to the aircraft. Tad and Buck are repairing it now. I guess we came out four or five hundred dollars ahead. Tad tell you what we hauled?"

"No. He just said you had a charter to Las Vegas and everything went okay."

"Good," Mike said.

"What?"

"Good. Good charter, Doris. No real problems."

"You ready for another charter, Mike?"

"Sure. The bird should be ready to fly by tomorrow morning. What kind of charter you talking about, Doris?" Mike shifted the telephone receiver to his left ear and picked up a ball point pen from the desk.

"An old friend of mine from Hollywood called last night. Actually an old friend of my late husband. Timothy Longshank. He's a—"

"Who? Longshank? Is that his name...or a description?"

"It's his name, Mike. Shame on you. He's a respected movie producer and director. I had a screen test with him a year ago...but I didn't get the part. I kept blowing my lines. Anyhow, he and his party are arriving tomorrow at noon. PSA flight from Los Angeles. He wants to fly down to Guaymas, Mexico for a few days. A fishing trip, I believe."

"Hang on a second, Doris. Let me check the *Airport Directory*." Mike pulled the publication from the shelf above his desk and leafed through the Mexico section. "Here it is. Guaymas International. Seven thousand seven hundred feet. Plenty of runway. Also international. We can fly there direct. How many in the party?"

"Five...plus their baggage and equipment."

"It'll be a full load but we can handle it. I want Tad to go with me. If we have any maintenance trouble down there, I don't trust the Mexican mechanics."

"Good. I'll tell him it's all arranged. He's a swell guy, Mike. You`ll like him. Probably ask you to go fishing with them."

Mike opened the office door and shouted to Tad Little. "Got

another charter for tomorrow, partner. Five passengers for Mexico. Some movie director and his pals. Going fishing in Guaymas. Put the seats back in and clean her up good."

November 26, at three minutes past noon, PSA flight 1101 from Los Angeles touched down at Phoenix Sky Harbor Airport. A pre-arranged airport limousine picked up the Hollywood party and delivered them to the Air Arizona hangar. Tad Little met the group as they departed the long, white Cadillac.

Mike Murphy, dressed in a crisp new white pilot shirt with epaulets and a slim, black four-in-hand tie, observed from his office window. A large-girthed man exited the limousine first. He must have weighed close to 300 pounds. His white shirt and khaki trousers were sweat soaked, his bald head and face sprinkled with scraggly black hair.

"Jesus Christ!" Mike said aloud. "Another baby bull."

Next out of the Cadillac was a short blonde male cherub in jeans and a sweatshirt with the arms cut off at the shoulders. He busied himself retrieving baggage and equipment from the trunk and baggage rack atop the vehicle.

Mike shook his head. Putting all that gear and five passengers in the Beechcraft would be like putting ten pounds of crap in a five pound paper bag.

Next, two beautiful women—one blonde and the other brunette—exited the limousine like two goddesses descending from heaven. The tall blonde, attired in tight fitting white shorts and a multi-colored halter, exposed her ample rear asset as she bent over to remove some object from the seat of the car. The brunette, shorter in stature but every bit as well endowed, wore tight leopard spotted black leotards with a loose-fitting purple blouse.

Mike did a quick double-take. He grabbed the *Playboy* magazine on the desk and ripped through the pages to the rear of the publication. There, in next month's coming attractions, stood a tall amply-endowed blonde next to a voluptuous brunette seated on a stool. He looked out the window again. From this distance the two looked very much like next month's *bill d'fare*.

The last to emerge was a slightly-built man with a dark complexion, pencil line mustache, long stringy black hair and dressed in black trousers and polo shirt. He wore dark eye shades, and a small black cigar hung from his lips. Tad offered his right hand to the man, as he had all the others, but the man kept both hands in his trouser pockets.

What a dirt-ball, Mike thought. He took another quick look at the magazine's coming attractions, then tossed it into a desk drawer and ambled out of the office to meet his charter group.

Tad Little greeted Mike and introduced him to Timothy Longshank. Mr. Longshank's large, sweaty right hand engulfed Mike's as the two acknowledged each other.

"Ah...Mikey," Mr. Longshank purred. "Doris told me so much about you, but she neglected to say how incredibly handsome you are. You should be in films. Let me introduce you to my good friends."

"A pleasure to meet you, Mr. Long–" Mike paused. "Mr. Longshank."

"Mikey, that's Phillip Lens." Mr. Longshank pointed to the chubby blonde man standing on the rear bumper retrieving equipment from the car-top baggage rack. "Best close-in camera man in the business."

Mike nodded. The man waved.

"This is Arturo Casanova," Longshank continued. "Arty's not feeling well. Something he ate, I suppose."

Mike nodded again. Arturo rolled the little black cigar from the left side of his lips to the right.

"And, Mikey, this is Dolores DeLabia." Mr. Longshank pointed to the dazzling brunette, then to the blonde, "And this is Bobbi Bleaugood." Each extended a hand to Mike.

Mike wanted to say so badly, *you must be shitting me!* "Understand you're gonna do a little fishing in Guaymas. Nice place ...good fishing. As soon as Mr. Little gets the plane loaded, we'll blast outa here."

AIR ARIZONA

"Adventure, Mr. Murphy. Adventure. That's what we`re looking for. A great adventure." Mr. Longshank threw his arms wide apart. Mike walked toward the Beechcraft. He motioned for Tad Little to join him. "Tad, you gonna be able to get all that shit in the airplane? I think we'll be a couple hundred pounds over-grossed."

"Buck's loading some of it now. I've never seen so much crap for one fishing trip. We'll have to secure some of it in the aisle between the passengers."

"That's illegal as hell, Tad. We get caught doing that and we'll be flat-ass outa business."

"Twenty-five hundred smackers, Mike...and all our expenses paid. Besides, did you see those two knock-outs?"

"I saw them. Look like two hundred dollar a night hookers to me. Okay, let's get loaded. I'll call over and file a flight plan."

At 1:25 P.M., Air Arizona One labored down the taxiway to Runway 26 Right for departure. Mike Murphy sat in the left pilot seat and Tad Little occupied the right copilot seat.

"Did you compute a final gross weight, Tad? What was it?"

"You don't want to know, Mike. When you get to normal takeoff speed let it pick up another five or ten knots before you try to pull it off."

The tower issued takeoff clearance while the Beech was still taxiing. Mike rounded the corner to Runway 26 Right with ten to fifteen knots taxi speed and slammed the throttles to the sea-level stops. The plane shuddered and began a slow acceleration.

"Let's get this fuckin' great adventure in the air...if we can!"

CHAPTER 7

A warm morning breeze greeted Mike Murphy as he opened the sliding glass door and walked out onto the small terrace overlooking the incredibly blue water of the Sea of Cortez. He and Tad had shared the more-than-adequate guest room at the Posada Hotel. It was early, a little after 7:00 A.M., and Mike had the remnants of a tequila hangover, the results of popping *slammers* with Tad Little in the hotel bar the night before.

Yesterday, they had flown Timothy Longshank and his party, a group of Hollywood weirdoes, from Phoenix to Guaymas, Mexico. Dolores DeLabia and Bobbi Bleaugood occupied the room adjacent to Mike and Tad. Mike had heard them come in late last night, laughing and slurring words that he could not understand. There were also male voices, but Mike did not recognize them as the male members of Mr. Longshank's group.

Mr. Longshank, Phillip Lens and the dirt-ball, Arturo Casanova, each had his own room in the plush hotel.

Mike lit a Camel cigarette, inhaled deeply, held it for several seconds, then exhaled slowly. I should know better, he thought, than to match Tad drink for drink of tequila. The sonofabitch must be a half-brother to Jose Cuervo.

Mike re-entered the room and placed his right foot on the bed containing the comatose Tad Little. He shook the bed violently. "Up and at'em, good buddy. It's almost time for Tequila Marys."

"What?" Tad rolled over on his back. "Jesus, Mike, I was having the best dream. Why did you wake me?"

"Making out with those two bimbos, I bet."

"I was making out with the blonde and the brunette kept trying to cut in to get her turn."

"Climb in a cold shower, Tad. I'm ready for some huevos rancheros."

There was a sharp rap at the door.

"Yes," Mike answered.

"Mr. Murphy," a voice outside said. "It's me, Phil Lens. Mr. Longshank wants to know if you and your friend care to join us on the boat this morning."

Mike slipped on a pair of blue jean trousers, then opened the door. "Tad and I were just going down to have breakfast."

"There's plenty to eat on the boat...rolls, coffee, fresh fruit. The limo's out front now waiting to take us to the dock."

"How about it, tequila buddy?" Mike said to Tad Little. "Want a great adventure this morning?"

"Not me," Tad answered. "I'm going down to the field and check on the Beechcraft. Those Mexicans will have all the equipment stolen if I don't keep my eyes on it. You go ahead, Mike. Hell...you may even catch a marlin."

Mike turned to Phillip Lens. "Tell Mr. Longshank I'll be happy to go fishing with him."

The boat nestled to the dock wasn`t your ordinary everyday fishing boat. It was a plush sixty-five foot cabin cruiser. Dolores, Bobbi and Arturo were already on board, as well as the Mexican captain. Phillip Lens had already made several trips to the boat this morning loading the equipment. He opened the limousine door and assisted the massive Timothy Longshank from the vehicle. Mike Murphy followed on his own.

"Great day for a fishing trip, Mr. Longshank," Mike said looking at the bright blue sky hovering over the deep blue water.

"A great day for a great adventure, Mikey. We'll have loads of fun."

The deep-throated engines fired up. Timothy, Phillip and Mike boarded the yacht. The lines were cast off, and the sixty-five footer slipped its berth and headed out of the harbor toward the white-capped sea.

"Mikey," Mr. Longshank placed his large right hand on Mike's shoulder. "Why don't you join the captain on the bridge. I've got some things to go over with Phil, Arty and the girls. Business things."

"Sure, Mr. Longshank," Mike replied. "Hard to get away from business, I know."

Timothy Longshank smiled, or more correctly, leered. "You have no idea of how many hard things I deal with in this business."

Mike joined the captain on the flying bridge. "Great day, isn't it, skipper?"

The captain grunted.

"Going for marlin?"

The captain grunted again and pointed at something ahead on the horizon.

The captain and Buck Skin would make great friends, Mike thought. Neither talked. They communicated by grunting and finger pointing.

The boat headed southwesterly until clearing a point of land, then settled on a northeasterly heading following the coastline. After forty-five minutes or so, the boat coasted into a small bay of an island, where the captain released the anchor which rattled out of its locker and secured them to the sandy bottom. Mike could see the bottom clearly, twenty or so feet below the keel of the cabin cruiser.

"A little bottom fishing, huh?" Mike said to the captain.

The captain uttered another grunt and pointed to the sandy beach at the apex of the small bay.

Timothy Longshank and his friends came out of the cabin. Phillip Lens sat up a tri-pod and attached a large movie camera to it. The girls, dressed in short cut-off jeans and white T-shirts each carried a small duffel bag. Their erect nipples and brown areolas were visible through the knit shirts. Neither wore bras. Arturo emerged bare-chested wearing only tight-fitting, white sailor trousers and white deck shoes.

Mike was puzzled. "Going to shoot some film of the fishing?" he inquired of Phillip Lens.

Phil ignored the question.

Mike turned to Timothy Longshank who was soaking wet with perspiration. He wore wash khaki trousers and a flowered Hawaiian shirt, with a baseball cap covering his bald head. In his hand he held a battery powered megaphone.

"Fishing?" Mike said weakly.

"Not fishing, Mikey. Filming. A great adventure. Sit back and enjoy."

Mike rejoined the captain on the flying bridge.

Phillip and Arturo lowered a small dinghy on the stern of the cruiser into the water, using the davits and hand operated winches. Phillip entered the dinghy and started the outboard motor. Arturo assisted Dolores and Bobbi with their bags into the small boat.

When they were seated, Arturo cast off the dinghy's line, and Phillip directed the craft toward the sandy beach.

Mike watched in amazement. He had never seen a movie being filmed.

Phillip deposited the girls on the beach and returned to the cruiser. He fiddled with the camera for a few minutes, then began shooting. He first aimed toward the beach where both girls were waving madly. Next he shot forward on the cruiser catching Arturo in the frame. Arturo pointed toward the beach and Phillip moved in for a close-up of him.

Next, Phillip and Arturo loaded the camera and tri-pod into the dinghy. They assisted Mr. Longshank into the dinghy, no small task, and followed after him. They cast off and headed for the sandy beach. Dolores and Bobbi still waved madly.

Mike could not make out what the figures on the beach were

doing. It appeared as if both girls were hugging Arturo Casanova and hanging all over him. He could make out Phillip Lens with the camera at some distance from the three, and Timothy Longshank standing behind the cameraman. He couldn't mistake Timothy Longshank. He looked like a beached whale.

Whatever they were doing took nearly an hour. Mike went below for coffee and rolls. In the cabin was a king-size bed with light purple sheets and two large purple pillows. Over the bed on the ceiling was a large mirror and another large mirror on the bulkhead beside the bed. Feeling that he had intruded into somewhere he didn't belong, Mike poured a cup of coffee from a thermos and took two Danish rolls. He went topside and joined the captain on the bridge.

The dinghy was enroute back to the cruiser. It skimmed quickly over the smooth water of the bay.

Reaching the cruiser, Timothy Longshank and Phillip Lens climbed aboard. Again, not an easy task. Arturo handed up the camera equipment to Phillip and departed for the shoreline again.

Phillip set up the camera and in a short time the dinghy was headed back for the cabin cruiser, this time with Dolores, Bobbi and, of course, senor dirt-ball. Mike and the captain watched intently. The camera rolled.

Secured alongside the larger boat, the girls exited the dinghy and climbed aboard the cabin cruiser. Mike could not believe what his eyes were telling him. Both girls were bare-breasted and wore only the smallest of bikini bottoms.

"Jesus Christ!" Mike uttered. "I don't believe it."

The captain grunted with a slight smile.

Arturo climbed out of the dinghy and boarded the vessel. Both girls threw their arms around him showering him with kisses, their hands exploring his hard thin body. He made his way to the cabin entrance dragging the nymphs with him.

The cameraman, equipment and *Moby* Longshank followed close behind. The cabin door slammed closed.

Mike took a sip of the now cold coffee. "Did you see that?" he said to the captain.

Another grunt.

Several minutes passed. Silence from the cabin...then a scream. "You sonofabitch!" one of the girls shouted. "I'm not ready yet."

More silence. Another scream.

"Cut! Cut!" yelled Timothy Longshank. "Goddamnit, Dolores, get with it. Get your ass over there."

"Screw you, dickhead!" a female voice sounded loudly.

"Don't screw me, bitch," Longshank screamed. "Screw him ...that's what you're getting paid for. Screw him!"

More silence.

The director spoke loudly again. "Get in there, Bobbi...hurry. No, no...not that way...the other way."

Mike wiped his brow. He was sweating profusely. The captain did not appear concerned.

Again the director shouted. "Get in there, Phillip...good tight shot. Again, Bobbi...faster. Goddamnit, Arty, you're losing it. Keep it up or we're gonna lose the whole fuckin' shot."

Again silence.

The cabin door burst open. Timothy Longshank exploded on deck. "Goddamnit!" he screamed. "Sonofabitch! That's what you get when you work with amateurs. Phillip, get out here. We're gonna have to shoot it over. That slimy sonofabitch doesn't know how to act a climax shot. We should have got Long John. This stupid wop's no porn actor."

Phillip patted Mr. Longshank's massive back. "It's okay, boss. I got some pretty good stuff. Let's give it another try. Bobbi's fluffing Arty up now. He should be ready in a couple of minutes.

The director shook his large head. "Okay, Phil, but that sonofabitch better not let me down again. I'll throw his ass overboard for shark bait."

The two re-entered the cabin.

There was more talking...whispers. Mike strained to hear the conversation. He could only make out an occasional word.

"...pearl dive—"

"...dog it—"

"...roll over—"

"... sorry, Mr. Longshank...it won't happen again."

"Okay, let's roll again. Action."

Silence from below. Straining, Mike could hear low moaning, an occasional groan, a gasp, a female panting, "More...more."

The captain continued to stare seaward. What was going on below didn't seem to faze him. Maybe he didn't understand. What was going on below was definitely fazing Mike Murphy. He conjured up pictures in his mind. There was a perceptible stirring in his loins—an enlargement of his manhood. A part of him wanted to look through the porthole to see what was going on...another part wanted to be far far away.

"No, goddamnit! No! No! No!" Mr. Longshank's voice boomed from below. The cabin door burst open again. This time it was Arturo who emerged. He was stark naked. He dashed for the rail at the stern. Hanging his upper body over the rail, he flung forth the contents of his stomach. This was followed by several minutes of dry heaving.

Timothy Longshank came out of the cabin flinging his cap to the deck and kicking it. It went over the side into the water. The top of his bald head was beet-red. "You slimy sonofabitch," he shouted. "You're through...hear me? You'll never work in skin flicks again. You're a goddamned fag...I knew it."

Phil also came out on deck. "Boss, we don't need much more. Just some close-in stuff."

Mr. Longshank rubbed his hairless head and gazed toward the sandy beach. Several minutes passed. He turned to face the flying bridge. "Mr. Murphy," he called. "Can you please come down here for a minute?"

Mike climbed slowly down the ladder not sure he wanted to be on the same level with the ranting wild man.

"Mikey, I need a big favor. I hate to ask but we need some help...big help. I'm willing to pay five hundred...no, a thousand. A thousand crisp green American dollar bills."

"For what?" Mike responded.

A wide, yellow-stained, toothy smile crept between the scraggly mustache and beard of Timothy Longshank.

"Oh, no!" Mike started backing up the ladder. "I can't—"

"Mikey...Mikey. Just listen, please. Let me give you the pitch."

Mike stepped back down on the main deck and stared directly at the massive mad man.

"These two broads...Dolores and Bobbi," Longshank continued, "have been dropped off on this desert island by a millionaire yachtsman because they wouldn't put out for him. He's big, fat and obnoxious."

A self-portrait, Mike thought.

"The girls won't have anything to do with him. But along comes this Latin-hunk of a sailor. He rescues them from the deserted island. To show their appreciation, they go all out with sexual favors ...anything he wants. A *menage-a-trois*. We're gonna have to rewrite after that. Write that wop fag out of the script. We only need a few more shots onboard the boat. Close ups. Phillip will shoot so that you'll never be seen above the shoulders. Just your body."

"Christ, Mr. Longshank, I can't do that. Someone might recognize me."

"Mike...most of my work is viewed outside the states. Overseas. No one will know you."

"I just don't think I can—"

"Why not, Mikey? You queer? Don't like girls?"

"No...of course not! It's just—"

"Did Mrs. Kissling tell you that we're real good friends? REAL GOOD FRIENDS! A few words from me, Mikey, and you can kiss your little silver airplane good-by. Are we communicating now, Mr. Murphy?"

"Yes, sir...we are. I just don't know if I can act and have sex at the same time."

"Act? You don't have to act, Mikey...just be natural. Let nature take its course. Just pull out when you're ready so we can catch it on film." Mr. Longshank pointed toward the cabin door.

Mike entered the cruiser cabin. Dolores and Bobbi lay naked on the purple bed. Dolores was polishing her nails and Bobbi nibbled on the edges of a stale Danish roll.

"Get your clothes off, handsome," Bobbi said. "Come lie down with us."

"We'll get you ready for the next shot," Dolores added.

The captain peered into the cabin through the open door. He grunted.

AIR ARIZONA

CHAPTER 8

The return flight from Guaymas was quiet. Mike Murphy stared straight ahead in a trance. Tad Little, in the copilot seat, sat with a smug grin on his face. The girls had told him how Mr. Murphy had helped them out in a pinch. Timothy Longshank perused a new script he had acquired. *Come Along With Me*, it was entitled. Arturo Casanova was not onboard the craft having elected to stay in Guaymas with his new-found love, a bus boy from the hotel restaurant.

Buck Skin met the Beechcraft as it taxied into the parking space beside the Air Arizona hangar. A limousine awaited the Longshank party. They had less than an hour to catch their PSA flight to Los Angeles. Buck and Tad began off-loading the equipment from the aisle to allow the passengers to deplane. Mike helped unleash the tie-downs.

"How's everything back here?" Tad inquired of Buck.

Buck answered with a grunt that usually meant *okay.*

With the passengers and equipment off-loaded, Tad and Buck began loading the limo. Mike started toward the hangar but stopped after a few steps and turned to the party waiting to board the vehicle. "Thanks for flying Air Arizona," he said.

Dolores and Bobbi ran quickly to him. Bobbi threw her arms around Mike and delivered a deep-tongue kiss. Dolores followed with a kiss on the cheek and a nibble on his ear.

"I love you, you big stud," Dolores whispered. "Come and see me sometime. You've only seen the tip of my iceberg."

Mike retreated to the confines of his Air Arizona office. He dug through the desk drawers and found the *Playboy* magazine. Turning quickly to the back of the issue he scrutinized the photo of next month's attractions.

"I don't think I'll have to buy next month's issue," he said aloud.

The phone rang. Mike let it ring three times before answering. He wasn't sure he wanted to talk with anyone just now.

"Mike." It was Doris Kissling calling. "You're back. Timothy called and said you'd be back this afternoon. How'd it go? Isn't Timothy just the greatest?"

Greatest what? Mike wondered. "A real keen guy, Doris. A little different, but just a real fine individual."

"Timothy said you helped them out with a film. A small part, he said."

"More like a big part, Doris." Mike paused. "You know what kind of films he makes?"

"Of course. Remember, I had a screen test for one of his movies?"

"Jesus, Doris...he makes skin flicks. Pornos. These two girls—"

"You mean Dolores and Bobbi?"

"You know them? You know Dolores and Bobbi?"

"Of course, Mike. Bobbi worked with me on my test. Dolores helped me—"

"I can't believe it, Doris. You tried out for a part in a porno film? They're pure filth."

"Mike, I'm disappointed in you. I thought you were more sophisticated. I thought you were...never mind. This is not what I called about. I've got good news for you."

"Not another charter flight for your friends, I hope."

"No. Not a charter. A contract. For a full year."

"A contract, Doris. With who? Doing what?"

"Cactus National Bank. It's the largest bank in the state. As it stands now, it takes them a full day...sometimes more, to get their funds and paperwork out and back to some of their outlying branches with an armored truck. I talked with Dave Peterworth and—"

"Hold it, Doris. This isn't another Longshank, is it?"

"No, Mike. Dave is the senior vice-president of Cactus. He was a close friend of J. P.'s—my departed husband. We worked out a contract for air service to Tuba City, Kyenta, Holbrook, Winslow and Payson." Doris Kissling was buoyant.

"How often, Doris? One...two times a week?"

"Every night except Saturday and Sunday...and if this works out, we'll get some more of their outlying branches. Isn't that just fabulous, Mike? I mean, really."

"Doris," Mike said angrily. "We can't run the Beechcraft every night. We need it for charters...some times two, three, four days in length. We can't tie it up every night."

"We don't have to. I bought another airplane. A Cessna 180...with a cargo-pack."

Mike let out a long low whistle. "That's a damn good airplane...if it's equipped with full instruments. There's some rugged flying country up north. I'm not even sure they all have lighted runways for night flying."

"They do...and it is. I've already checked that all out. The contract begins in two weeks."

"Wait a minute, Doris...not so damned fast. Who's gonna fly this new bird? I`m pretty busy with the Beech."

"Got that worked out too."

"Not another friend of J. P.'s, I hope." Mike chuckled.

"A friend of mine, Mr. Murphy. A good friend. Buzz Bigsby."

Mike exploded. "You mean the jerk that flies traffic patrol for KCRP in the mornings...and disc-jockey's that wild-ass music in the afternoons?"

"You know him, Mike. I didn't know that you—"

"I don't know the sonofabitch and I don't want to. I'm the director of operations for this air service, you know? I interview and hire the pilots. You just put up the money."

"Good, Mike. He'll be there about nine-thirty in the morning for an interview. You'll love him. Bye!"

Ten o'clock came. No Buzz Bigsby. Ten-thirty. Mike Murphy sat at his desk dressed in dark blue trousers, a freshly pressed white pilot shirt and black tie—befitting the director of operations and chief pilot of a two-plane air charter service. He crushed out the half-smoked cigarette in a tray on his desk.

Tad Little opened the office door and entered. "Look real sharp there, Mr. chief pilot. Not making another movie, are you?"

"Damn you, Tad. You don't have a clue to what's going on around here, do you? You don't know Jack Shit!"

"I know Jack Shit, Mike. I worked for him at the Plymouth-Dodge dealership for a year. Him and his two brothers...Hot and Dip. I know a lot of shits, Mike."

Mike smiled. "Sorry, old buddy. Doris has got me going ape-shit. She's bought another airplane...a Cessna 180. She wants me to interview some jerk-off friend of hers to fly it."

"Yeah, I know," Tad said. "She called me last night and told me to hire a couple more mechanics. Think I should?"

"She's paying the bills. I guess we don't have a whole lot of choice."

The office door swung open. "Either one of you dudes Mike Murphy?" The speaker was a short heavy-set young man in his mid-twenties. His face was pock-marked and his stringy blonde hair hung to his shoulders. He wore a pale yellow polo shirt with KCRP emblazoned across his chest in bold blue letters. He wore soiled leather Mexican sandals.

Tad Little pointed at Mike.

The stranger walked to the desk and thrust his right arm forward. "Hey, man, I'm Buzz. You know, the KCRP Buzz." He put his fist to his mouth simulating a microphone. "Hey there, all you hipsters. You don't wanta be messing with Central Avenue this morning. There's a three block back-up at Thomas Road heading south." He brought his hand down. "You know? That Buzz."

"Have a seat Mr. Bigsby." Mike pointed to a chair beside the desk.

"Hey, no one calls me Bigsby...just Buzz." He turned to face Tad Little. "You must be that other dude Doris told me about. Little...something."

Tad smiled, excused himself and left the office.

"Well, Mr. Bigsby...I mean, Buzz. Understand you're looking for a flying job with Air Arizona. What are your qualifications?"

"My what?"

"Your qualifications. Your flying experience. Hours. Things like that."

"Doris said you just bought a new Cessna. Hell, I've got all kinds of experience in Cessnas."

"One-eighties?" Mike asked.

"One-fifties," Buzz replied. "I've got nearly five hundred hours in those puppies."

"What other aircraft have you flown? Anything larger than a one-fifty?"

"No...just one-fifties. That's all I've ever flown. I know the bird inside and out."

"The one-fifty's a pretty small airplane compared with the one-eighty...plus the one-eighty's a tail dragger."

"A Cessna's a Cessna, Mike. Mind if I call you Mike?"

Mike signaled his okay with a nod.

"You just add another five miles an hour to the landing speed for each model you go up. You didn't know that?"

"How about credentials, Buzz? What license and ratings do you hold?"

"Commercial. I had to have that for the traffic job. Single engine ...land. No water stuff. Working on my instrument rating now."

"You'll need an instrument rating. The weather can get pretty wild up north. Have much night experience, Buzz?"

"I'll have my instrument rating by next week. Got a few hours night time...maybe ten."

"Did Doris tell you that this is mostly night flying? Gets dark up there on the Indian Reservations. Clear dark night...easy to get vertigo."

"Hey, Mike, I can do it. Been a doer all my life. I can fly anything, anywhere, anytime. Just give me the opportunity."

"You'd have to quit your job with KCRP."

"I'll quit the morning traffic flying. Plan to keep the afternoon DJ gig. Doris said it would be okay. I'm off the air at five. Plenty of time to get out here and fly the round-robin."

Mike stood at his desk. "Thank you, Mr. Bigsby. I'll let you know in a few days."

"You mean I don't have the job? Doris said the interview was just a formality. I've already told the station to get a another morning traffic guy."

"I'll let you know. Now please excuse me."

Buzz Bigsby started toward the door. "Dig you later, Mike," he said, then departed.

Mike Murphy was steaming. His fist and jaw were in a clinching contest...neither had the advantage over the other. They were deadlocked in a bone-shattering tie, both about to burst. "That sonofabitch!" he finally screamed. "That miserable, slimy, rotten sonofabitch!"

Mike sat a full five minutes staring at the wall. Finally, he slid the telephone across the desk and dialed.

"*Keesling reseedence.*" a Hispanic female voice answered.

"Mrs. Kissling at home? Mike Murphy calling."

"*Si, shee's* home. *Shee's* at her morning bath. *Un momento, por favor.*"

A minute elapsed. Mike detected another receiver being lifted.

"Hello, Mike. So good of you to call. What did you think of Buzz? A real sweetheart, isn't he? Best DJ in the valley."

"Goddamnit, Doris! The guy's a flake...a fruitcake. He'll pile up our new Cessna the first time he climbs into it. We need a professional pilot, Doris...not some puddle-jumping wannabe."

"Mike, he's been flying for two years. Never had an accident ...except the time he hit some high power lines out by Mesa. It wasn't his fault. They just strung them the day before and no one told him."

"Jesus, Doris. I think we're just asking for trouble if we hire him. I'd rather—"

"Mike, I pay the bills...and a hell of a lot more. Now hang up. Call Buzz. Tell him he's hired."

The Beechcraft was in the air almost every day: a small group of Swiss tourists over the Grand Canyon; a wealthy business tycoon and his girlfriend to San Diego and back for dinner at her favorite restaurant; a group of contest winners sponsored by a large appliance dealer on a sight seeing flight over the valley; a ruthless real estate developer taking photographs of Northern Arizona nothingness which would surely be advertised as OWN YOUR OWN RANCH IN ARIZONA, $300 DOWN AND $35 A MONTH; an honest-to-goodness fishing trip to Mexico. Tad flew only occasionally with Mike in the Beechcraft, utilizing his time to hire and check-out two new mechanics for the bank flights.

At 5:30 P.M., December 9, 1957, Buzz Bigsby arrived at the Air Arizona hangar. It would be the first flight of the Cactus National Bank contract. Mike had flown the Cessna several times to become familiar with it and had planned to take Buzz on an orientation flight on the 8th, but a last minute charter negated the orientation ride.

Buzz was dressed in his Levi cut-offs, a grease-stained windbreaker and his dirty Mexican sandals.

Mike was furious. "Goddamnit, Buzz...you look like a scumbucket. Tomorrow I want you dressed in a white pilot shirt, dark trousers, black shoes and a tie. Understand?"

Buzz nodded that he did.

"Also," Mike continued, "I thought you would be here earlier. I wanted to take you around the field for a few touch-and-goes. Get you a little familiar with the one-eighty."

"Hey, Mike, everything's cool. No sweat. I can handle it...trust me."

An armored truck from Cactus National Bank pulled up beside the silver and turquoise Cessna. Buck and one of the new mechanics began loading the contents of the truck into the cargo pack underneath the fuselage of the one-eighty.

Mike handed Buzz a clipboard with a number of pages attached. "Here's your flight plan, Buzz. I had to file instruments because of light snow showers around Holbrook and Winslow. It's a five hour and twenty-one minute flight including thirty minutes on the ground at each airport. You'll need to refuel in Winslow. I've already advised them you'll require fuel. You may want to top-off again in Payson if the weather's bad back here in Phoenix. It's forecast for rain at about midnight. All the navigation equipment is in the plane—enroute charts, approach plates, airport directory. Tad will have the cargo manifest for you at the airplane that'll tell you what bags go off where. You shouldn't have to re-compute your weight and balance unless you pick up some fairly heavy stuff. Try to put it in the center of the cargo pack. Questions?"

"Can't think of a thing, Mike. Looks like you've got it all covered. Be back about midnight."

Mike's reply was stern. "I'll be here...and listen, Buzz, don't push it. If the weather gets rotten, land somewhere VFR or head back to Phoenix. I don't want you to spread our new aircraft and a half-million dollars of Cactus Bank's money across the Northern Arizona landscape."

Buzz grinned, then put his right hand palm upward toward Mike. "Five, man. Catch you on the flip side."

"Five," Mike responded as he slapped Buzz's outstretched hand.

Air Arizona Two was airborne at 6:35 P.M. It turned northward and continued climbing. Mike called Pulliam Airport in Flagstaff.

"What's the weather like up there?" he asked.

"Light snow showers. Visibility about five miles. Light icing reported below ten thousand feet."

"Thanks," Mike replied with obvious concern.

At 9:00 P.M., Mike called Winslow Municipal Airport to remind them that the Cessna would be in later for refueling.

A man with a slow cowboy drawl answered. "We'll gas him...if he gets in. Weather's gettin' real shitty up here." At 10:30, Mike called Winslow again to see if Arizona Two had arrived. He was informed by the operator that the telephone lines to Winslow were down and that it would be several hours before they could be repaired.

At 11:15, he called the Payson Airport. There was no answer. Mike called out to Tad Little who was working on the Beechcraft. "He must be down somewhere, Tad. Weather up there's real nasty. I know I shouldn't have let that dumb-ass disc jockey fly our airplane. Doris has got us in barrel of shit again."

Tad shrugged his shoulders and kept on working.

At 11:15, Mike called Phoenix Approach Control. "You guys have any reports on our Cessna one-eighty?"

"He's on short final now," replied the controller.

Right on time. "I'll be a sonofabitch!" Mike shouted. He yelled out to maintenance again, "Tad. Two's on short final. Should be in the blocks in about five minutes."

AIR ARIZONA

CHAPTER 9

Each weekday evening in December, 1957, except for the 24th and the 25th, The Cessna 180, designated Air Arizona Two, skipped dutifully around Central and Northern Arizona—Tuba City, Kayenta, Holbrook, Winslow, Payson and Phoenix. Rain, sleet, hail, snow nor dark of night deterred or delayed its appointed rounds. Buzz Bigsby, dressed in dark trousers, white pilot shirt, black tie and highly polished black leather boots, with hair trimmed neatly, piloted the little craft fulfilling the Cactus National Bank contract.

For the first week of operation, Mike Murphy remained at the Air Arizona office until the Cessna 180 was on final approach for Phoenix Sky Harbor Airport. Each evening he fully expected the phone call that would inform him that Air Arizona Two was down somewhere along the route. The call never came and after the week, Mike stopped sweating the disc-jockey-pilot and accepted him as a professional.

Mike continued to fly the Beechcraft on charter operations when scheduled. With the increased responsibilities in maintenance, Tad Little was no longer available to ride in the copilot seat on the charter flights. Although only one pilot was required for the craft, it was helpful to have another set of eyes in the cockpit, especially in heavy traffic areas. Buck Skin had flown several times with Mike, but Mike couldn't tell if his grunts indicated he saw another aircraft or he was just agreeing with something he had said.

With Doris Kissling's concurrence, Mike hired another pilot in mid-

AIR ARIZONA

January—a retired navy lieutenant commander with over a thousand pilot hours in Beechcraft C-45's. Harvey Khule was a seasoned veteran with twenty years of flying experience. Nothing fazed him. He had seen it all. Buzz Bigsby dubbed him *Commander Cool*. The nickname stuck.

Commander Cool flew both the Beechcraft and the Cessna. He frankly admitted he was not working for the money but for the sheer pleasure of flying. He had a perpetual smile on his face and flew every hop he was scheduled without a quibble or hesitation.

More and more, the tempo of operations required Mike Murphy to be in his office. It was not what Mike wanted. He loved the flying, but the handwriting was on the wall, so to speak—the schedule board was full of commitments. Doris had suggested purchasing another Beechcraft. They had turned down a number of charters because Air Arizona One had scheduled missions, and soon an increase in Cactus National Bank's pick-up and deliveries would require another single-engine aircraft. This meant more pilots, more mechanics, more staff and office personnel. Mike's dreams of flitting around the country in the converted C-45, hauling neat little packages, pouches of courier mail, hunting and fishing parties, and sweet young things in short skirts or skimpy shorts was gone. Air Arizona was growing rapidly. It was fast becoming a major operator requiring major management and that, Doris Kissling had reminded him, was the job of the director of operations. Mike threw out the wooden chair and surplus desk that had served him from the beginning and purchased a new large oak desk and over-stuffed office chair. He ordered an adjoining office to be constructed and hired an attractive twenty-five year old strawberry-blonde secretary. He hoped she would wear short skirts or dresses.

On March 7, Mike Murphy received a phone call from Buzz Bigsby. It was eight o'clock in the morning.

"Hey, Mike...did you hear the news?"

"What news? I don't know what you're talking about, Buzz."

"I won. I'm the disc jockey of the year. It's on page seven of the morning *Arizona Republic*."

"You mean the national disc jockey of the year? That's great."

"No...not national. Arizona disc jockey of the year. Arizona Broadcaster's Association is giving me the award at their banquet tonight."

"That's great, Buzz. Congratulations."

"Thanks, Mike...but I do have a problem. Can you get Commander Cool to take the bank run tonight?"

"Impossible, Buzz. He's in Albuquerque with a charter."

"Crap! I really wanted to go tonight...but I guess I can pick it up some other time. Thanks anyhow."

"Go to the banquet, Buzz. You deserve a night off. I'll take the bank run this evening. I need to get some air time. My butt's becoming part of the office furniture."

At 5:30 P.M., the armored truck arrived at the Air Arizona hangar. Buck Skin supervised the loading of the Cessna 180. Two newly-hired service personnel retrieved the heavy bags from the truck and placed them in the cargo pack of the single-engine aircraft.

Earlier, Mike had checked the weather and filed an instrument flight plan for the scheduled route. The weather across the state was clear but the IFR flight plan guaranteed him constant surveillance and tracking by FAA radar facilities.

At 6:25, Air Arizona Two lifted from Runway 26 Right and turned northward to intercept the Victor 327 airway to Flagstaff. From Flagstaff, Mike would receive radar vectors to Tuba City for landing.

His route took him just east of the small town of Sedona and over Oak Creek Canyon. A bright full moon illuminated the towering rock formations in and around the canyon. The canyon was his favorite spot in all of Arizona, and he had spent most of his summers as a youngster at his aunt's cabin, mid-way up the narrow canyon near the location where Zane Gray had lived and written his *Call of the Canyon*. Mike had fished for trout and swam, and found adventure after adventure hiking the many trails where sweet ripe apples and tart-tasting blackberries were abundant.

Reporting his position over Flagstaff, Mike received a vector of 005 degrees magnetic with clearance through the restricted military airspace north of the city.

At 7:10, with clearance from the Denver FAA center, Mike began a visual descent to the 4,966 foot elevation Tuba City Airport. As cautioned by the Airport Directory, he maintained constant vigilance for people or animals on the runway. The Tuba City Airport was not your run-of-the-mill everyday kind of airport.

The stop at Tuba City was routine. The bank delivery van was beside the runway when Mike landed. Ground time was less than twenty minutes. The off-load at Tuba City exceeded the onload by nearly four hundred pounds. Mike was airborne on takeoff in less than eight hundred feet of runway distance.

Departing on Runway 1 to the north, he climbed to nine thousand feet and reported his departure to Denver center. Denver confirmed his position by radar and reported no known traffic along his route.

The bright full moon was now high in the sky and cast an eerie luster on the landscape below. Wildcat Peak to his left stood majestic in moonlit splendor and a sprinkling of lights ahead defined the small community of Cow Springs. This was Navajo Indian country. Further north, near Kayenta, was Monument Valley, the hallowed homeland of the Navajo people. To the east was the Hopi Indian Reservation with its sacrosanct First, Second and Third Mesas. He would over-fly this reservation on the Kayenta to Holbrook leg of his flight. This area of Arizona was the site of many bitter feuds between the Navajo and Hopi tribes, and the interference of the federal government in no way lessened the bitterness.

The stops at Kayenta and Holbrook were as routine as the Tuba City stop. Mike was twenty minutes ahead of schedule. With this dispatch he should arrive back at Phoenix before 11:30 P.M.

At 9:38 he lifted from Runway 21 and flew over the city of Holbrook on the short leg to Winslow. Two more stops and he would be home.

At Winslow, Mike greased the Cessna 180 onto Runway 29 and taxied to the service ramp for refueling. He relished the opportunity to fly again, especially on such a beautiful night. He assured himself he would find more opportunities to fly rather than spending his time hassling over aircraft and pilot schedules, fees and revenues, customer satisfaction—all the headaches inherent in operations management. Mike was not cut out for that. He was a pilot pure and simple. He would talk to Doris about hiring a non-flying manager, and Mike could concentrate more on being the air service's chief pilot.

The fuel truck pulled up beside the Cessna. The driver stepped out of the cab and called to Mike, "You Mike Murphy?"

"Yeah," Mike replied.

"Better call Phoenix. A Tad Little called a few minutes ago. Said it was important to call him right away."

Mike ambled to the fuel shack. "Use your phone?" he said to the man at the counter.

The man nodded.

Mike dialed the number for his office in Phoenix.

Tad Little answered. "Hey, Mike...good you called. I tried to reach you in Holbrook but you had just taxied out."

"What's up, Tad? The fuel man said it was important to get a hold of you."

"Right. We've got two passengers at Winslow for you. They should be there shortly. You need to bring them directly to Phoenix. Don't stop at Payson. I've cleared it with the bank. They know you're skipping Payson tonight."

"What's the big hurry, Tad? These some kinda VIP's?"

"Sort of. The lady's the daughter of an Indian chief. Some kinda honcho in their tribal government. She's about to give birth—"

"She's what?"

"About to have a baby, Mike. There's some kinda problem. I don't know what...but they can't handle it in Winslow. Her old man's here in Phoenix and wants a specialist to handle the delivery here. An ambulance will be waiting for you at Sky Harbor."

"The other passenger her doctor?"

"No, Mike. It's her medicine man. He—"

"Goddamnit, Tad! Sounds like another baby bull to me. How do you get into these things?"

"Mike, it's important. Her father's a good friend of Doris."

"Shit! Every weirdo in the country must be good friends of Doris."

Mike slammed down the phone and walked dejectedly back to his aircraft. As he approached the plane, an ambulance with flashing red lights pulled up beside the Cessna. The fuel man removed the nozzle from the left tank and secured the tank cap. He returned the fueling hose to the reel on the truck and handed Mike a clipboard with the fuel bill attached. Mike signed the invoice and tore off the receipt for his records.

The ambulance pulled forward, then turned and backed to the entrance door on the right side of the craft. The driver exited the vehicle and moved quickly to the rear of the ambulance. He opened the doors outward. A spine-splitting scream erupted from inside the ambulance. It was followed by a series of sobs...and then another ear-shattering scream. A large lump formed in Mike's throat.

A tall man leapt from the rear of the ambulance. He was dressed in buckskin clothing and moccasins. A large silver concho belt was secured around his waist with a turquoise decorated silver necklace adorning his neck. Assisted by the driver, the two men removed a wheelchair from the rear of the vehicle. In—or more properly—all over the wheelchair sat a young Indian woman weighing some two hundred-fifty to three hundred pounds. She was also dressed in buckskin, a large sack-like garment covered her body, and her long black hair hung nearly to the ground. Her large brown eyes were opened wide in a gesture of sheer terror. Her chest heaved in several convulsions and another piercing scream came from her mouth.

Mike pointed to the entrance door of the Cessna 180. Thoughts of a baby bull flashed through his head. He estimated the young woman's girth to be some ten to twelve inches wider than the aircraft door.

The ambulance driver and the medicine man wheeled the yammering young woman to the aircraft. Together they lifted from the wheelchair and inserted her into the cabin door. On the count of three, by the driver, the men lunged mightily into the back of the buxom woman literally popping her into the aircraft. Another nerve-jangling caterwaul. Mike winced. The driver entered the Cessna and assisted the lady to a seat behind the pilot seat. The medicine man shot back to the ambulance where he retrieved a small drum and mallet.

The driver, apparently drained of energy, exited the aircraft slowly. He shook his head then walked sullenly back to the ambulance.

Mike climbed into the pilot seat and quickly ran through the *engine start* checklist. The fuel truck driver gave Mike an exaggerated thumbs up, smiling broadly. Mike returned the gesture with the middle finger of his right hand, then hit the starter switch.

The medicine man entered the aircraft and squeezed into the seat beside the gargantuan mother-to-be.

Mike taxied speedily to the runway for takeoff. The medicine man began striking the drum with the mallet and chanting. Mike wheeled the aircraft onto the runway and instantly gunned the engine to full power. The young lady let forth a tremendous screech. The medicine man quickened the tempo of the drumbeat and chant.

"Let's get this great fuckin' adventure in the air," Mike said under his breath.

He kept the nose high in the air climbing at 85 mph, the maximum rate of climb speed. He leveled at 10,000 feet, the minimum enroute altitude for Victor airway 95—the most direct route to Phoenix. He lit a cigarette and reported his departure to Albuquerque Center. "Albuquerque Center, Air Arizona Two, out of Winslow, level ten thousand."

"Roger, Air Arizona Two. We have you in radar contact fifteen miles south of Winslow tracking on Victor nine-five. Would you like a higher altitude, sir?"

"That's negative, Albuquerque. I'm requesting minimum enroute altitudes and no flight path deviations to Phoenix. I have a semi-emergency."

"Roger, Air Arizona Two. Please state the nature of your emergency."

"Albuquerque, you're not gonna believe this...but I've got a squalling squaw about to deliver a baby which I believe is breached, and an Indian witch-doctor pounding on a goddamned drum and chanting incantations. Please advise Sky Harbor I'm estimating there at 2305 local. I want an ambulance and a doctor to meet us on the runway. Copy?"

"Roger, Air Arizona Two. You are cleared to the Phoenix VORTAC for an approach to Sky Harbor Airport. Maintain minimum enroute altitudes. Report all altitude changes to Albuquerque Center. We'll notify Phoenix. Good luck. *Via con Dios*."

The shrieks subsided to low moans. Mike extinguished his cigarette and slipped on his oxygen mask. Regulations required its use above 5,000 feet at night. He glanced in the rear view mirror and saw that the woman had closed her eyes and was breathing deeply. The tempo of the drumbeat slowed. The passengers were feeling the effects of the low oxygen content of the cabin air. Mike was not about to tell them to put on their masks. The lack of oxygen was better than a sedative.

Mike was thankful for the smooth night air. He turned down the cabin air temperature control a few degrees. The cabin was already cool, but Mike was soaked with perspiration.

He could see the lights of Payson just ahead of the aircraft's nose. Further ahead, over a ridge, he could make out the loom of lights from the Phoenix area complex. Both passengers rested quietly. Light turbulence shook the craft as the steep Mogollon Rim slipped beneath them.

"Yeowwwww!"

Mike sat up abruptly in his seat.

"Yeowwwww!" Even louder.

Mike turned to see the young girl attempting to stand. Her breathing was labored, punctuated with shrill shrieks.

The medicine man dropped to his knees and disappeared under the buckskin skirt.

A moment later he reappeared. "Baby come," he said.

"Baby can't come now, goddamnit! Not now," Mike shouted.

"Baby come...now! You help." The medicine man lifted the lady`s left leg and placed it over the pilot seat forcing Mike to duck under it. He pulled the buckskin skirt up above her waist. Another shattering scream erupted from the woman.

The medicine man extended her right leg to the adjoining seat. Mike reached above his head and turned on the bright white cabin light. He could see that the woman wore no undergarments. Blood-stained fluid oozed from the vaginal opening.

The medicine man spoke in his native language. The girl nodded and bore down hard, grunting loudly as she did. Mike could see something emerging from the opening, something with a deep crevice. He hoped it wasn't the baby's head.

"Air Arizona Two, Albuquerque center. We show you drifting right of course. Are you experiencing any difficulty?"

"Affirmative, Albuquerque. The patient is delivering now."

"Air Arizona Two, maintain ten thousand feet until passing Tonto Intersection, then cleared to eighty-five hundred feet. Contact Phoenix Approach Control on 120.7 passing Tonto."

"Air Arizona Two, roger clearance. Out." Mike rolled in left aileron and rudder to return the craft to the proper heading. The aircraft had descended to 9,500 feet. He increased the power and started a climb back to 10,000. The white cabin light had destroyed his night vision. Outside everything was black. He turned his attention back to the young Indian. The crevice he had seen was the baby's buttocks.

"Must turn baby now...bad this way," the medicine man said. He took a powdery substance from a leather pouch hung round his neck and sprinkled it over the young woman. He intoned another prayer.

Another loud long scream.

AIR ARIZONA

The medicine man went to his knees again. This time he pushed the soon-to-be mother upward. "Mr. pilot," he cried. "Turn the baby."

Mike turned in his seat to a kneeling position and faced the spread-eagle legs of the young woman. He slid his hands around the buttocks of the infant and pushed gently inward.

"Air Arizona Two, Albuquerque center. We show you drifting far left of course. Over."

Mike could not answer. He knew the craft was turning left and climbing. A quick glance to the instruments assured him the bank and climb were gentle. He continued to push and rotate the baby in the birth canal. Suddenly the baby's leg thrust from the opening.

"Air Arizona Two, Albuquerque center. Do you read?"

The medicine man nodded then smiled. "That way okay. Not right way...but okay."

Mike thrust his hand in further and grasped the baby's other leg. He pulled it gently and it too emerged. Holding both feet, he continue to apply light pulling pressure.

"Air Arizona Two, Albuquerque center. We show you reversing course. If you read us, please reply."

A horrendous scream was emitted from the young mother. The baby popped from its containment right into Mike's hands.

"Air Arizona Two, Albuquerque center. Check your altitude immediately. We are losing radar contact."

Mike took another quick look at the instrument panel. The bank had increased significantly and the unwinding altimeter indicated a rapid descent. The Cessna had entered a graveyard spiral. Mike handed the baby to the medicine man sitting on the floor and turned back in his seat to control the aircraft. The altimeter read 7,500 feet...well below the minimum altitude for the area. Mike rolled the wings level and brought the nose upward. The airspeed was 205 mph—approaching the never-exceed speed of the Cessna.

The plane began climbing smartly with the airspeed dissipating rapidly. He observed the magnetic heading—010 degrees...nearly the reciprocal of the intended course. He rolled into a steep left bank and when the airspeed had dropped to 120 mph, he applied full engine power.

"Aircraft in the vicinity of Payson, Arizona, this is Albuquerque center. We have lost contact with a Cessna one-eighty. Please report any sightings of explosions or fire on the ground."

Mike continued to turn until the VOR instrument in the cockpit centered indicating a return to Victor 95 airway. He keyed the radio switch and transmitted. "Albuquerque center, this is Air Arizona Two. Over." Mike continued climbing back to the assigned 10,000 feet of altitude. Mountains in the area peaked to nearly 9,000 feet.

"Air Arizona Two, Albuquerque center. Say your position please."

"Roger. Air Arizona Two is climbing on Victor ninety-five to ten thousand feet."

"Roger, Air Arizona Two. You had us scared there for a few minutes. What happened?"

"The patient delivered...right into my hands. I guess we got turned around and lost some altitude."

"That's affirmative. We were tracking you right into the side of the Mogollon Rim. Do you require further assistance?"

"Negative, Albuquerque. We'll continue on to Phoenix."

Another loud cry...but from the baby. Mike looked back to see the medicine man tying off the cord with a leather strip which had held the medicinal pouch around his neck. The man severed the umbilical cord between the two ties with a hunting knife. He looked up at Mike and smiled broadly. The mother also smiled and closed her eyes.

The Cessna passed through the imaginary point in the sky labeled Tonto Intersection on the navigational chart. Mike eased off the power starting a gradual descent. He keyed his radio microphone. "Phoenix Approach Control, Air Arizona Two, Tonto, descending to eight thousand five hundred ."

"Roger, Air Arizona Two. Radar contact over Tonto. Maintain visual flight. Contact Sky Harbor Tower on 118.7 at ten miles. The ambulance and a doctor are standing by."

Mike rogered the clearance and turned back to see how the

passengers were doing. He heard a large thunk. The medicine man grunted. Mike knew the placenta had just delivered. Tad's clean-up crew would have their hands full tonight.

CHAPTER 10

On April 4, 1958, the owners of Air Arizona came together for the first time in an organized stockholders' meeting. The meeting was held in the board room of the Copper State Bank in downtown Phoenix. In attendance was Doris Dushane Kissling, president of Air Arizona; her attorney, Regis Rothchild; Michael Murphy, director of operations; and Thadeus Little, director of maintenance.

Mrs. Kissling called the meeting to order. "Gentlemen, the first annual meeting of Air Arizona stockholders is now in session. I have invited Mr. Regis Rothchild, who is not a stockholder, to act as recorder and legal advisor. He served my late husband for many years as his legal representative and now serves me in the same capacity."

Mike and Tad each nodded a signal of recognition to the attorney, who nodded back. The men had not previously met.

"First, I have a few announcements," Doris continued. "Due to the heroic action of our chief pilot, Mr. Murphy, a baby boy was born to Mary Littlefeather last month in the cabin of our Cessna one-eighty over Payson, Arizona. In Mike's honor, the boy has been named Michael Murphy Littlefeather. He is the grandson of one of the most important Indian leaders in our state."

Mike took a sip of coffee from the cup in front of him. He hoped no one saw the obvious blush on his face.

Tad signaled Mike with a thumbs up.

"Next I would like to announce the purchase of three additional aircraft to be added to our inventory." Doris shuffled through the stack of papers before her on the table. "We will take delivery early next month of a Beechcraft Model E-18-S. This new aircraft will be delivered to our hangar by a factory pilot. The contract includes a week of familiarization and check flights of all Air Arizona pilots.

"Two new Cessna Model one eighties will be ready for pickup in late May. These, along with our existing one eighty, will be utilized for our bank courier service. Regis has negotiated contracts with three more major banking institutions for pickup and deliveries to a number of smaller communities throughout the state.

"Mike, I want you to prepare a plan detailing the number of pilots and support personnel we will require to operate our new equipment. I need that by next Friday. We need to advertise and start hiring by the first of the month." Doris shuffled through some more of the papers. "Additionally, Mike, I want to remind you that you are the director of operations. I want you in the office working...not flitting around the country in one of our aircraft. Limit your flying to your duties as chief pilot...flight and line checks."

Doris turned to Tad Little. "Tad, I want you to submit a plan, also by next Friday, outlining the personnel and equipment you'll need for our new increased tempo of operations. If we can get work done cheaper and as quickly using outside facilities, that's fine...but I want a dollar and cents comparison before we obligate to an outside company."

The room was quiet except for a slurp of coffee taken by the attorney. Mike and Tad stared at Doris in disbelief.

"Gentlemen," Doris said, "I know this is not exactly what you had in mind when you proposed the start-up of an air service. This is not what I envisioned either. However, I see a lucrative future in aviation in the state of Arizona. This is just the beginning. If either of you is not comfortable with this expansion, I am ready and willing to purchase your share of the corporation. Mr. Rothchild has prepared a statement of our net worth as of this date. I can have the cash in your hand within an hour of notification. If you desire to stay and move forward under my direction, you are welcome to do so. I cannot believe that you both will not become millionaires within five to six years. With this increased responsibility, I am prepared to double your present salary. I might remind you, Mike Murphy and Tad Little, your original investment in this corporation was damned little." Doris Kissling stood. "Questions?"

Silence.

"Then I make a motion that these proceedings be closed."

Silence.

"Do I hear a second?" Doris stared directly at Mike Murphy...then at Tad Little.

"Seconded," Tad blurted out.

"Good. As president of Air Arizona I close the first annual meeting of stockholders." Doris retrieved the folder of papers on the table. "By the way, off the record. Regis has investigated the procedures for becoming a scheduled airlines. I'm confident that by early next year we will be able to provide regularly scheduled passenger flights to major cities in Arizona, Nevada and Southern California. I have purchased the options on five Convair three-forties." Doris paused. "Good day, gentlemen."

She stood to leave the room. Regis and Tad also stood. Mike remained seated.

"Shit!" Mike Murphy said aloud. "Shit! Shit! Shit!"

Doris stopped, looked back over her shoulder and smiled. "Mike, I still have the account at Durant's. Just tell the bartender to put your drinks on my tab."

During the week of May 5th, Mike interviewed and hired six additional pilots. He hired a non-flying administrative assistant and three *gophers*—go for this—go for that.

Tad hired three aircraft mechanics and three airframe specialists. The engine mechanics would work directly for him and the airframe specialists would work under Buck Skin. He also hired three *gophers.* He contracted all major engine overhauls to Aerodyne Aviation.

AIR ARIZONA

On May 12th, the new Beechcraft E-18-S arrived from the factory in Wichita, Kansas. All Air Arizona pilots received familiarization flights and a check ride from the company pilot.

On May 30th, Buzz Bigsby and Commander Cool picked up the two Cessna 180 Skylane II's at the factory and flew them to Sky Harbor Airport in Phoenix.

On June 2, Lieutenant Junior Grade Michael M. Murphy, USNR, sent a letter to the Chief of Naval Air Reserve Training requesting reassignment to a reserve jet fighter squadron. Much to Mike's surprise and delight, he received orders to an F9F-6 Cougar reserve fighter squadron based at Los Alamitos. One weekend each month Mike could tear up the skies over Southern California in a hot navy jet fighter plane. The fun returned to flying.

AIR ARIZONA

CHAPTER 11

On January 5th, Air Transport West convened its first Convair 340 class of 1959. The school, located at the Oakland International Airport, offered classes in initial, refresher and ATP (Air Transport Pilot) in several commercial transport aircraft. The thirty pilots in the Convair 340 Class designated 59-01, included twenty-one employees of Air Arizona.

Mike Murphy, Air Arizona's chief pilot, was enrolled in the initial course. Ten of the Air Arizona pilots were taking the refresher course —they would serve as copilots for the newly chartered airline, and the other ten, already qualified Convair 340 pilots, were taking the ATP Course and would become captains. The ATP endorsement was an FAA requirement to fly as captain for a scheduled airline. Mike was the youngest of the twenty-one pilots and had the lowest number of pilot hours. He could not qualify for an ATP rating until he had logged two hundred fifty hours in the Convair 340. The three-forty was a big step up from the small twin-engine Beechcraft in which Mike had logged all his multi-engine pilot time.

A call from Doris Kissling early last November had instructed Mike to start interviewing pilots for a planned April 1st start-up of scheduled air passenger operations. She said the Air Arizona office and hangar spaces at Sky Harbor Airport would be tripled in size with construction starting immediately, and that ticketing and baggage facilities were being constructed in Terminal One at the airport.

"Doris," Mike had said during their conversation, "what are we going to do with the charter business...the Beechcrafts and Cessnas?"

"On the first of April, Mike, the Cessnas and the Beech 18 will be transferred to Bigsby Air Services. The old Beech will be—"

"Whoa! Run that by me again, Doris."

"Bigsby Air Services. Buzz is leaving Air Arizona to start his own company. Another little capital venture I'm undertaking. Commander Cool and the other pilots we have now will be going with Buzz to the new company."

"What the hell will I be doing, Doris?"

"Mike, you're the director of operations and chief pilot for Air Arizona Airlines. I want both you and Tad with me. We're gonna build the best damn regional airlines in the country. Who knows?...we may even go national...or international someday."

"Doris, I'm not really sure we—"

"Mike, my offer still stands anytime you want it. You can have your share in cash within an hour. Should be plenty to start another little one-plane air service. Just let me know."

"No, I'm with you, Doris. Just seems like we're moving a little too fast. Do the pilots know yet?"

"Buzz does...of course. So does Commander Cool. You can tell the others. I don't think any of them will complain...since they're all getting a sizable pay raise in the deal."

"What about the old Beech, Doris? The C-45."

"We're gonna mount it on concrete and display it right in front of our office. It'll remind us how far we've come."

Mike did not reply. He started to hang up, but then said: "Doris...just how much fuckin' money do you have?"

On March 16th, the first of the refurbished Convair 340's arrived at Sky Harbor. It was painted silver with the turquoise trim and tail design that Buck Skin had applied to Air Arizona One less than two years before. Two others arrived on March 17th and the fifth on the 18th.

AIR ARIZONA

On March 27th, an open house was held in the newly completed hangar spaces of Air Arizona Airlines. In addition to the Governor of Arizona and other distinguished guests, reporters from every major newspaper in the state and every major television station were in attendance. Doris Kissling proudly climbed the stairs leading to a platform at the forward end of Convair 340 number N58791 and broke a bottle of expensive French champagne over its nose. Nothing broke or fell off!

AIR ARIZONA

CHAPTER 12

Wednesday, April 1 (April Fool's Day), 1959 at 8:00 A.M.—right on schedule—Air Arizona Airlines Flight 4101 taxied from Terminal One, Phoenix Sky Harbor Airport to Runway 26 Left. In the pilot seat was Captain William Hanna, an airline veteran with six thousand plus hours of flight time—more than two thousand in Convair 340's. In the copilot seat was First Officer Brad Dunbar, an ex-Air Force pilot with nearly four thousand total hours. In the jump seat, between the two pilots, sat Air Arizona Airline's chief pilot and director of operations, Michael Murphy, the proud possessor of a piddling 1750 pilot hours.

As they taxied into the run-up position for 26 Left, they passed in front of a silver and red Beechcraft E-18-S. Large black letters the side of the silver fuselage proclaimed: BIGSBY AIR SERVICES. Commander Cool was in the pilot seat of the Beech 18. He snapped a sharp military salute as the Convair taxied by, and Mike responded with a thumbs up.

Flight 4101 was the inaugural flight for Air Arizona Airlines. Its scheduled route was Yuma, San Diego, Burbank, Oakland, Reno, Las Vegas and return to Phoenix. Another flight crew was pre-positioned in Oakland to relieve the Phoenix crew who would remain overnight in Oakland. Tomorrow this crew would take Flight 4201 from Oakland to Reno, Las Vegas and Phoenix. In addition to the three pilots in the flight compartment, two female flight attendants and forty-one passengers were situated in the cabin.

AIR ARIZONA

Three other Air Arizona Airlines flights were scheduled for the day —4102, 4103 and 4104. Flight 4103 was scheduled for a 4:00 P.M. departure and would fly the same route as the 8:00 A.M. flight. Flight 4102 would depart at noon and 4104 at 8:00 P.M. and fly the route in reverse order. All Air Arizona Airlines' flights for this day were booked to near-capacity, the result of an unheard of low fare.

Captain Hanna positioned the Convair in the run-up area and completed the engine run-up procedures and the *before takeoff* checklist.

Mike observed the veteran pilots executing the required checks and completing the necessary actions. A jump seat pilot was not required for Convair 340 passenger flights, but as chief pilot, Mike was observing the pilot's performance. He would do so on a regular basis to insure company procedures were being followed. It was a difficult task for him since all company pilots had not only more flight time in the Convair, but also more overall flight time than Mike. Even so, the company pilots treated him with deference and respect knowing that his opinion and evaluations would insure their continued employment with the dynamic young airline.

The captain and first officer completed the required checks and were ready for takeoff. Brad Dunbar called Sky Harbor Tower for takeoff clearance. Bill Hanna pressed a button in the cockpit that alerted the flight attendants to take their seats.

"Arizona 4101, Sky Harbor Tower. You are cleared for immediate takeoff on Runway 26 Left. Wind is 200 degrees at ten knots. Contact Phoenix Departure Control on 119.2. Good to have you with us."

Captain Hanna directed the silver and turquoise Convair 340 onto the runway. "With your permission, Mr. Murphy, Flight 4101 is ready for takeoff."

Mike nodded. Bill Hanna released the brakes and pushed both throttles full forward. The Pratt and Whitney Double Wasp R-2800 engines snarled and the aircraft accelerated down the runway.

Lost in the engine's roar was Mike Murphy's comment: "Let's get

AIR ARIZONA

this great fuckin' adventure in the air."

AIR ARIZONA

CHAPTER 13

Captain Hal Fogarty taxied the Convair 340 onto Runway 27 and aligned the nosewheel with the white line down the center of the runway. "Your aircraft, Mike. I'll handle the nosewheel steering to V-One."

Mike Murphy, seated in the copilot seat of Air Arizona Airlines Flight 1601, took the control yoke in his right hand. "My aircraft. Tell the tower we're rolling." Mike advanced the throttles with his left hand until the engine manifold pressure gauge registered thirty inches on both engines.

Captain Fogarty keyed his microphone and transmitted. "Lindbergh tower, Arizona Zero-One is rolling Runway Two-Seven."

"Roger, Arizona Zero-One. Contact San Diego Departure Control on 125.3 after airborne."

Mike released the brakes and smoothly applied full throttles to the engines. The Convair accelerated rapidly.

At eighty knots, Captain Fogarty called out, "V-1, releasing nosewheel steering."

"Roger," Mike responded, now using rudder pressure alone to maintain the aircraft on the runway centerline.

At 118 knots indicated airspeed Mike eased the control yoke back toward his lap. The nose of the Convair rotated about fifteen degrees upward. A moment later the main wheels broke free of the runway. Mike raised the nose a few more degrees. "Gear up," he

71

called.

From the pilot seat, Hal Fogarty positioned the gear lever to *Up* and the aircraft wheels retracted into their compartments.

"Flaps up," Mike said. "Rated power...water-alcohol off."

The Naval Training Center pistol range slipped under the nose of the aircraft three hundred feet below.

The Captain selected 125.3 on the VHF transceiver. "San Diego Departure Control, Arizona Zero-One is off Lindbergh for your control."

"Roger, Arizona Zero-One. Radar contact. Continue present heading to intercept Victor 363, then flight plan route. Climb to and maintain eight thousand feet. Contact Los Angeles Center at Krauz Intersection."

Captain Fogarty repeated the clearance to San Diego Departure. "I'll take the aircraft now, Mike. Nice takeoff. Go ahead and dig out the approach plates for Burbank. They're down to about two miles visibility in smog. We'll probably get an ILS to Runway 33."

"Thanks for the takeoff, Captain. I'm getting to feel very comfortable in the three-forty. I want to get as much seat time as I can. It's a little embarrassing being the chief pilot with so little time in the aircraft."

"You're doing a great job, Mike. The flight crews all like and respect you. You guys turned a fly-by-night air service into a respectable regional airlines."

Since the inaugural flight in April of 1959, Mike had taken every opportunity to fly as copilot in the Convair. He was anxious to obtain the two hundred fifty hours necessary to upgrade to captain, the proper rating for an airline chief pilot. His flights as copilot were in addition to his duties as director of operations and chief pilot. Twelve to eighteen hour work days were not uncommon.

Mike dug through the brown leather navigation bag to locate the instrument approach plates for the Burbank Airport. Out of the window to his right he could see the Southern California coastline north of La Jolla, and the large kelp beds just off the shoreline. It was a cloudless day but a thick haze restricted forward visibility. Visibility was good only when looking vertically down or up.

Captain Fogarty leveled the Convair at eight thousand feet and set cruise power manifold pressure and RPM to maintain two hundred forty knots indicated airspeed. He engaged the autopilot. "Time for a few minutes relaxation before we start down again."

Mike keyed his radio microphone. "San Diego Departure, Arizona Zero-One is level eight thousand. Estimating Krauz at four-seven. Pomona next."

San Diego Departure rogered the transmission. Mike retrieved the clipboard from the nav-bag and entered a notation on the Trip Report Form. *Off Lindbergh at 1030 local 1/6/60 on time. 40 pax, 8 bags U.S. mail.*

"Hal, I show us passing the 270 degree radial of Oceanside. Looks like we'll be about a minute early at Krauz."

"Good, I show us right on Victor 363. Go ahead and put Pomona on the number two VOR. Inbound course of 344."

Mike tuned the VOR navigational radio to 110.4 and identified the Morse Code dots and dashes as POM, the code for the Pomona VOR transmitting station.

The course needle in the number two VOR edged toward the center. When centered, Hal Fogarty turned the aircraft right to a heading of 340 degrees. "Give L. A. Center a call, Mike. Request radar vectors to an ILS final."

Mike set 135.5 frequency in the VHF transceiver. "Los Angeles Center, Arizona Zero-One is at Krauz, eight thousand feet. Destination Burbank. Request radar vectors to ILS final approach."

"Roger, Arizona Zero-One. Radar contact at Krauz. Contact Burbank Approach, 134.2, at Prado for radar vectors. Maintain eight thousand. Caution, heavy military traffic in the vicinity of Marine El Toro."

"Mike, put Paradise on the number two VOR, 256 radial," Captain Fogarty said. "Keep a sharp eye out for those wild-ass Marines out of El Toro."

"Roger, Hal. I can see the air station just off to the right. I'll—"

"Jesus! What was that?" Fogarty yelled out. "Something just shot by right in front of us. Looked like an A-Four. Tell L. A. we've just had a near-miss. Tell them—"

A loud crashing noise came from the right side of the Convair. The aircraft pitched violently upward and to the left.

"Goddamnit! We've been hit. See anything out there, Mike?"

"No...but something sure hit us." The aircraft began a rapid roll to the right.

"Get on the yoke with me, Mike. Help level the wings."

Mike grabbed the control yoke with both hands and turned it hard to the left. Slowly the Convair rolled to wings-level flight.

"Hal," Mike screamed. "The airspeed's falling off fast. We're about to stall."

"Help me push forward...the controls seem jammed. We've got some major damage somewhere."

The cockpit door flew open. "Captain!" It was the senior flight attendant. "The whole right wing is missing from the engine outward...it's gone."

"Goddamnit! One of those Marine A-4's must have hit us. Can't see anything in this haze."

With Mike Murphy's help, the nose lowered allowing the airspeed to increase. The aircraft rolled right again entering a descending spiral.

"Left yoke, Mike," the Captain shouted. "Give me full power on the right engine."

Mike used his right hand to twist the yoke and his left to shove the propeller control to full RPM and the right throttle full forward. Slowly the aircraft returned to wings-level but was still descending.

Captain Fogarty shouted to the flight attendant bracing herself in the cockpit doorway. "Angie, tell the passengers to get in their seats now and tighten their seat belts as tight as they can get them. We're going down." He turned to Mike. "Tell L. A. what our problem is. We'd like to land at El Toro, if possible."

"Mayday! Mayday! Mayday! Arizona Zero-One is seven thousand feet over El Toro. We've had a mid-air collision and have lost our right wing from the engine nacelle outward. Requesting immediate landing at El Toro."

"Arizona Zero-One, Marine El Toro Tower is reading your mayday on guard channel. Switch immediately to Coast Approach Control, 132.7. We'll notify Los Angeles Center."

Mike reset the VHF transceiver. "Coast Approach, Arizona Zero-One with an emergency...seven thousand feet just south of Marine El Toro."

"Roger, Arizona Zero-One. We read your mayday on guard channel. Say your type of aircraft and souls on board."

"Coast, we're a civilian Convair three-forty with—" Mike paused momentarily, "with forty-four souls on board...two forward and forty-two aft. We've lost our right wing from the engine outboard. Do you have any other collision reports?"

"Arizona Zero-One, that's negative. We did have a Marine A-4 flight report severe turbulence at about eight thousand feet over El Toro."

"That severe turbulence was us. You'd better contact the flight and tell them to land immediately. One of them must have severe structural damage."

"Roger, Zero-One. Can you maintain altitude?"

"Negative, Coast...about two hundred fifty feet a minute down is the best we can do." Mike looked at Captain Fogarty who nodded his approval.

"Understand, Zero-One. Make a gradual one-eighty turn to the left for a GCA approach to El Toro."

"Coast, we'd rather turn right, if possible. We've got full left aileron in now and damn near full power on our right engine to hold a steady heading."

"Roger, Zero-One. Commence a gradual right turn and descend to two thousand feet. Contact GCA on 135.2. Return to this frequency if no contact."

Hal Fogarty eased back the right throttle to 35 inches. With the aileron full left, the Convair began a gentle right descending turn.

Mike changed radio frequency. "El Toro GCA, Arizona Zero-One is in a right turn descending through six thousand feet. We're about two to three miles south of El Toro."

"Roger, Zero-One, we have you in radar contact. Continue your right turn to a heading of 345 degrees...descend to two thousand. The field is closed to all traffic and crash crews are standing by. You'll have a rescue helicopter in your six o'clock position slightly above you. Understand there are forty-four souls on board...two forward...the rest aft."

"That's affirmative," Mike responded.

"Roger, Zero-One, this is your final controller. Do not acknowledge further transmissions. Continue your turn to 350 degrees descending to two thousand feet."

"Mike," Captain Fogarty shouted. "We're coming up on 350 now. Give me forty-five inches in the right engine."

"Forty-five," Mike answered. He moved the right throttle forward until the manifold pressure gauge read 45 inches. Both Hal and Mike continued to hold full left aileron.

"Arizona Zero-One, GCA. I hold you on course well above glide slope. Descend to two thousand as rapidly as possible."

Captain Fogarty reduced the left engine to idle. "Give me thirty inches on the right, Mike."

Mike decreased the right throttle to 30 inches. The Convair dropped like a rock. Mike could hear the screams from the passenger compartment over the sound of the engines.

"Now, Mike, forty-five inches." Fogarty increased the left engine to 30 inches. Mike responded with 45 inches on the right engine. The rapid descent slowed at 1,800 feet.

"Arizona Zero-One, GCA. You are down and on glide slope. Continue a normal rate of descent. Come left to 340 degrees."

"Shit! We haven't got any more left aileron," Fogarty yelled. "Get on the left rudder with me, Mike. Kick the sonofabitch! We'll skid it over."

Mike pushed the left rudder pedal with all his strength. The aircraft's nose skewed left.

"Hold it, Mike...hold it. Okay, now ease it out."

Mike released the pressure he was applying to the left rudder pedal. The nose came back to the right.

"Arizona Zero-One, GCA. Good correction. I hold you on course and glide slope...two miles from touchdown. For your information, we just received a report that one of our A-4's crashed near Twenty-Nine Palms. The pilot reported a control malfunction and ejected. We believe it's the aircraft that struck you."

"Roger," Mike replied.

"Mike, we'll land with no flaps. Hold the gear until we're sure we'll make the runway. If we miss the runway I want to go in wheels up." Captain Fogarty activated the crash alarm in the passenger cabin.

"Mike, you handle the right engine. Use whatever power is necessary to keep us wings-level and nose-straight. I'll handle the controls and left engine."

"Arizona Zero-One, GCA. We have you on course and slightly above glide slope at one mile. Do you have the runway in sight?"

"Affirmative...runway is in sight." Mike eased off a few inches of manifold pressure.

The Convair crossed over the end of the runway at 200 feet.

"Give me the gear now," Captain Fogarty shouted.

Mike actuated the landing gear handle dropping the nose and main wheels from their compartments. "I show three down and locked, Hal."

"Good. Ease off a few more inches and we'll put this big sonofabitch down on the runway."

The Convair eased to the runway a thousand feet past the approach end. The touchdown was surprisingly gentle.

"No reverse," Fogarty said. "We'll let it coast to a stop."

Fire and crash trucks followed the slowing aircraft on both sides of the runway. When it came to a stop, fire crews rapidly converged on both side of the craft. Captain Fogarty pulled both mixture levers to *Off*, stopping the flow of fuel to the engines causing them to stop. He secured the magnetos and activated the folding stairs forward of the left wing.

The passengers filed off quickly. Some knelt to kiss the ground, others crossed themselves or glanced skyward offering thanks. A few went to awaiting ambulances, but most boarded a large gray bus marked U. S. MARINE CORPS AIR STATION EL TORO.

Mike followed Hal down the stairs. "Nice landing, captain. I didn't think we had a chance."

"That was no landing, Mike...it was a controlled crash. It scared the shit out of me...and I'm fearless."

They walked to the right side of the aircraft. From the engine nacelle outboard, there was no structure—only a few dangling wires, cables and aluminum piping.

"This is one that I'll put in my *great fuckin' adventure book*."

"What's that, Mike?"

"Nothing, Hal...nothing at all. Why don't you stay here with the aircraft until we know what they're gonna do with it. I'll bum a ride to Operations and give the company a call."

CHAPTER 14

Headlines in the Thursday, January 7 edition of the *Arizona Republic* proclaimed: MIRACLE LANDING AT CALIFORNIA MARINE BASE SAVES LIVES OF 40 AIRLINE PASSENGERS. The article praised the skills of the two Air Arizona Airlines' pilots for successfully maneuvering and landing the severely damaged Convair 340 after being struck by a Marine Corps attack aircraft.

Mike Murphy and Hal Fogarty returned to Phoenix Sky Harbor Airport on January 8, aboard Air Arizona Airlines Flight 1082. They were met by a bevy of news, radio and television reporters. Each question asked of Hal Fogarty was answered by: "Mr. Murphy here is our chief pilot. He can answer that for you."

The reporter's attention quickly focused on Mike.

"Who was piloting the plane at the time of the collision?"

"Captain Fogarty was in the pilot's seat. I was in the copilot's seat."

"Who actually flew the aircraft?"

"Captain Fogarty and myself both flew the plane. It required both of us to maintain control."

"Did you see the aircraft that struck you?"

"No, not the one that hit us. We did catch a glimpse of one of the other aircraft in the formation."

Hal Fogarty eased himself out of the circle of news reporters and darted to the Air Arizona office.

"Were you frightened by the possibility of an impending crash?"

"There wasn't time to be frightened. We relied on the excellent training all Air Arizona pilots have received in handling emergencies."

Questions and answers were battered back and forth for a half hour. Finally, Mike waved his hands above his head. "Ladies! Gentlemen! Please. We'll have a full news release available to you this afternoon. I need to get back to work. Thank you."

Mike pushed his way through the jostling crowd. Questions were still coming from all directions. Airport security guards blocked the entrance to the Air Arizona office, allowing only the chief pilot to enter.

He brushed quickly through the reception room into his personal office. Seated at his desk were Doris Kissling, Tad Little and Hal Fogarty. On the desk were bottles of gin, tequila, Scotch and Chardonay wine. On the screen of the large television set in the corner of the office a female reporter was summing up the live news conference with the Air Arizona Airlines chief pilot.

"Welcome home, Mike." Doris Kissling raised her glass of wine in toast. "Excellent job with the reporters."

Tad Little, with a glass of tequila, and Hal Fogarty, with a glass of Scotch, joined in the toast.

"Mike," said Tad Little, "you always were full of bullshit."

Doris poured a full glass of Beefeaters gin and pushed it across the desk to Mike. "I know it's not proper to consume alcohol in the office of the chief pilot, but I figured you needed a stiff drink. We all do. We really dodged a bullet on this one."

"You're not kidding, Mrs. Kissling." Hal drained his glass of Scotch and poured another one. "That landing at El Toro was ninety-nine percent luck and one percent skill. We just happened to fall out of the sky right over the runway."

"Well, anyway," Doris said, "the public believes we have the best damn pilots in the business. That sure won't hurt our revenue. Do you know that I have already had three telephone calls from producers wanting to purchase the rights to make movies about the incident?"

"Not Timothy Longshank, I hope." Mike set down his empty glass. "That sonofabitch will have us screwing the flight attendants on final approach."

Doris smiled. "I know two actresses who would enjoy playing the parts."

"So do I." Mike refilled his glass.

In February of 1960, the National Transportation Safety Board released its findings on the mid-air collision. Pilot error on the part of the A-4 Skyhawk was deemed the primary cause of the incident, aggravated by poor horizontal visibility and the necessity for the military pilot to maintain constant visual reference to the other aircraft in the formation. It lauded the actions of the Convair 340 captain and first officer for safely landing the seriously damaged airliner without loss of life or injury to the passengers, or to others on the ground.

The lengthy repairs required on the damaged Convair made it necessary for Air Arizona to obtain an additional aircraft to meet the scheduled requirements. Mike Murphy suggested leasing a Convair 340 since there were a number available for short term lease. Tad Little agreed. Doris Kissling had a different idea. She directed Mike Murphy to purchase two Convair 340's and have them painted the silver and turquoise color scheme of the other company aircraft.

"Jesus, Doris," Mike said. "We only use the fifth airplane as a backup. I can't see buying two more. The wounded bird will be back by mid-March. A short term lease would—"

"I've got something on the burner, Mike. Something I can't discuss now. If it goes through, we`ll need at least two more aircraft."

"More pilots too, I suppose."

"At least four more crews. You had better start looking through applicants again, Mike, and get the word out we'll be hiring."

"Shit! Here we go again. Another friend of J. P.'s?"

"As a matter of fact...yes." Doris turned to Tad Little. "Tad, we'll need—"

"I know, Doris. More maintenance personnel. I'll take care of it."

On February 17, 1960, Air Arizona took delivery of two refurbished Convair 340's. One was immediately put into the rotation for the California-Nevada-Arizona runs. The other was designated for pilot training, and Captain William Hanna, with the new title of senior instructor pilot, flew two training flights daily instructing the newly hired flight crews, and refreshing and upgrading the other company pilots.

On March 22, the repaired Convair 340 was returned to Air Arizona`s inventory, ready for service.

On April 3, Air Arizona Airlines commenced daily service to Tucson, El Paso, Albuquerque and Farmington. Six of the Convairs were now in daily use, the seventh reserved as a backup in the event of a mechanical failure or to replace an aircraft undergoing scheduled maintenance.

Mike Murphy's workdays became even longer with less and less time in the cockpit. Managing the operations of the fast-growing airlines was comparable to working two full-time jobs. Captain Hal Fogarty assumed the title and responsibilities of chief pilot. Mike was relegated strictly to directing the airline's operation. He eventually accumulated 250 pilot hours in the Convair 340 and was designated a captain. The title was in name only. He did not fly as captain for Air Arizona Airlines. He eagerly looked forward to the one weekend a month and the two week period in the summer when he reported for duty with Naval Air Reserve Fighter Squadron VF-872.

CHAPTER 15

"Good morning, Mr. Murphy. Here's the morning mail." Sheila Legge placed the large pile of envelopes on the desk before the director of operations. "Want some fresh coffee? I just made some."

"No, Sheila, thank you. I've had four cups already. That's enough for me."

The buxom blonde secretary exited the office, her long shapely legs exposed mid-thigh in a tight fitting short skirt.

"The only thrill I get anymore out of this business," he had told Tad Little, "is when Sheila sits down and crosses her legs to take dictation. I often dictate letters that never get mailed."

"You know, Mike," Tad Little had responded, "she doesn't wear underwear."

"How do you know that, Tad?"

"I know. Each time she walks out of your upstairs office onto the grating over the maintenance spaces, every mech in the place makes a mad dash for the tool boxes under the grating. They get better beaver-shots than you'll ever get in your office."

Mike Murphy sifted through the pile of correspondence. He placed the letters in three piles—one for matters he felt required his attention, one for his administrative assistant and one for the chief pilot. Some he simply tossed into the waste basket beside his desk. The last letter in the stack was addressed to: LTJG MICHAEL M. MURPHY, USNR.

Mike ripped open the envelope bearing his navy title. It was a

AIR ARIZONA

form letter.

> VF-872 Pilots:
>
> This letter is to inform you that this year's active duty training period (1 August through 12 August 1960) will be conducted at NAAS Fallon, Nevada.
>
> The facilities at NAAS Fallon will provide us with air-to-air and air-to-ground weapons training.
>
> All squadron members are to report to NAS Los Alamitos not later than 0600 hours, 1 August 1960. Squadron pilots will be assigned to fly our F9F-6 aircraft to NAAS Fallon.
>
> Unassigned officers/enlisted personnel will be flown to NAAS Fallon by a Reserve R5-D transport aircraft.
>
> I know you are as anxious as I am to receive this invaluable live ammunition training.
>
> C. L. Johnson
> CDR USNR
> Commanding Officer

"Hot damn!" Mike shouted. He pushed the lever on his inter-office squawk box. "Sheila! Get in here."

Sheila Legge rushed through the office doorway. "Yes, sir."

"Sheila, take a letter."

The attractive secretary opened the notebook in her hand and sat in a chair beside Mike's desk.

"Not there, Sheila. I want you right in front of me where I can see...I mean, where you can understand exactly what I say." Mike rose from his desk and slid a straight-back office chair directly in front of his desk six feet away.

The young lady moved quickly to the chair and sat down. She

crossed her legs before Mike could return to his chair behind the desk. "Are you ready?" Mike asked.

Sheila put her pen to the note pad and nodded.

"I'm going to say this just once...loud and clear. Make sure you get it."

"Go ahead, Mr. Murphy."

"To whom it may fuckin' well concern. I, Lieutenant J. G. Michael M. Murphy, USNR, will leave this fuck-all office in ten days for a full two weeks of flying and frivolity. I will be in the air where I fuckin'-A belong and happier than a pig in shit."

Sheila Legge's mouth dropped open. Her pad and pen fell to the floor, her glasses slid down her nose, her legs uncrossed and she sat there un-ladylike with knees wide apart.

"Goddamn you, Tad Little! You lie," Mike shouted at the top of his lungs.

LTJG Mike Murphy rode the naval reserve airlift R5-D from Phoenix to NAS Los Alamitos the evening before having to report for active duty training. The four-engine passenger/cargo aircraft was flown by naval reserve pilots each weekend from Los Alamitos to Las Vegas, Tucson, Phoenix and back to Los Alamitos to pick up the weekend warriors. On alternate weekends the flight was made in reverse order. Mike was pleased that this evening the final leg of the flight went from Phoenix direct to Los Alamitos.

The navy's old workhorse bumped, twisted and shook its way through numerous thunderstorms and heavy showers from the Colorado River near Blythe to the Santa Rosa Mountains east of the Los Angeles basin. Had this been a commercial flight, an assuring voice with a slow drawl would be saying over the cabin speaker, "Ladies and gentlemen, I need to ask you all to return to your seats now and fasten your seat belts. We have a little ol' area of light turbulence ahead which we should clear in a few minutes. Nothing serious. I'll turn off the seat belt light when we're all clear. Sure wanta thank you for flying *Dip Shit Airlines* this evening, and we'll do all we can up here to make it enjoyable."

Not so on the navy bird. One never knew if the pilot was a seasoned airline veteran putting in his reserve time or a Sears and Roebuck shoe salesman with less than a thousand hours of flight experience.

Two male enlisted flight attendants scurried about the cabin passing out barf bags to those with raised hands. Mike sat quietly. He was used to the turbulence in this area during the summer months— he had flown through it time and again—but it was never a comfortable experience sitting back in the cabin.

Following one particularly sharp drop the pungent odor of high octane aviation fuel filled the passenger compartment. The R5-D always smelled of fuel fumes—most all of them had leaky fuel cells— but this exceeded the norm.

The cockpit door flew open, and a squat gorilla-like man darted quickly back to a window over the wings. His sweat stained, grease and oil soaked flight suit identified him as the R5-D flight engineer. With a flashlight he peered out the round window at the starboard wing of the craft, and after a few minutes, moved to the other side and looked over the port wing. Apparently satisfied there was not a problem with the wings or engines he tripped his way over the feet of several passengers to the cabin area where the wing roots abut the fuselage. He popped open several buttons and pulled down the quilted lining on the cabin interior. Here he inspected the spaghetti of aluminum piping and fittings. Leaving the area opened, he returned to the flight compartment closing the door behind him.

In a few minutes the door opened again. This time the gorilla was followed by a tall slender youth apparently in his late teens or early twenties. At first Mike thought that maybe one of the pilots had brought along his teen-aged son allowing him to wear a navy flight suit, but as the youngster slipped his hand and arm into the exposed plumbing of fuel and hydraulic lines, Mike realized this was one of the pilots...maybe even the aircraft commander.

Mike took an extra-tight tug on his seat belt. The slender pilot removed his hands and shrugged his shoulders. The pilot and mechanic spoke to each other, their voices lost in the constant roar of the four reciprocating engines. The pilot shook his head, no. The engineer shook his head, yes. This continued for nearly a minute. Finally the pilot pivoted to return to the cockpit, his head still shaking from side to side.

The engineer threw both arms above his head as if to say, "Fuck it!"

Mike squeezed another half-inch grip out of his seat belt. He yearned for his single-seat F9F-6 aircraft where he made all the decisions and a *fuck it!* could be resolved by pulling the ejection seat handle over his head.

The Skymaster continued to bounce, twist and yaw. Lightning was visible through the windows on both sides of the aircraft, and Mike heard the sound of heavy precipitation impacting the skin of the craft. Unbelievably, a substantial number of the navy passengers onboard slept, their heads hung down near their chests. Maybe they're praying, Mike reasoned. Had he been on good terms with a deity of any of the world's known religions, he too would offer an invocation.   Ten or so minutes later the turbulence eased. Mike could see more and more lights from the ground below. He realized that they were over the mountains and descending toward Los Alamitos. A thin layer of low clouds were below them, thickening as they approached their destination. The aircraft headed for a particularly bright spot in the overcast. Mike knew the reason. Pilots flying out of Los Alamitos kept an ace in their back pocket, the un-approved, and certainly illegal, *Disneyland Approach*. On such nights when a thin overcast covered the area, and requesting an instrument clearance and approach from Los Angeles Center meant a holding delay of thirty or more minutes, pilots located Disneyland, the brightest-lit patch in the overcast, and after circling the area once to determine that they were the sole aircraft contemplating the approach, dove through the cloud layer on a heading of 260 degrees magnetic and reported to Los Alamitos Tower that the field was in visual contact and that they were requesting a landing.

The R5-D touched down softly on the runway with a noise which sounded to Mike like a great sigh of relief. Before the aircraft came to a stop on the ramp in front of Operations, the flight engineer had his tool box opened and was tightening fittings in the exposed area.

Mike rose from the hammock-like bench he had been sitting on for more than two hours and moved forward with the other passengers. Before exiting the aircraft, Mike stuck his head into the crew compartment door. The youngster was seated in the left pilot seat. A much older pilot sat in the copilot seat. He appeared to be asleep. Mike put his hand on the right shoulder of the young pilot. "I bet you guys are glad to be through for the night. The weather's pretty crappy."

"I wish," the pilot said. "We've got another run down to San Diego, Yuma and back. They've got some real shit down there."

CHAPTER 16

Mike Murphy arose early on the morning of 1 August. He had slept in the NAS Los Alamitos BOQ. Skipping breakfast, he was at the VF-872 operations office at 0600. The squadron spaces were already a beehive of activity. A list posted on the office door specified which squadron pilots were assigned to fly the Cougars to NAAS Fallon. Several of the pilots were already in their tan flight suits and were preparing to depart. Mike was the junior pilot by rank in the squadron and did not expect to see his name on the list, but he had hoped that it might be. A quick check of the names confirmed his suspicion. His name was on a second list — the list of officers and enlisted scheduled to ride the Reserve R5-D to Fallon. Its scheduled departure was 0800.

Mike returned to the BOQ officer's mess and ordered a breakfast of ham and eggs. He lingered in the mess, drinking coffee and reading the morning edition of the *Los Angeles Times*, until 0730 when he walked the short distance to the air station's flight operations building.

LTJG Mike Murphy, attired in his summer khaki work uniform and carrying his blue B-4 bag, joined the line of squadron personnel boarding the R5-D Skymaster. At the top of the boarding ladder an enlisted loadmaster was checking off the names of the passengers as they entered the aircraft. Mike noted that it was the same plane he had flown in from Phoenix on the previous evening. Seeing one of the

R5-D pilots peering into the wheel well located in the port inboard engine nacelle, Mike put his bag down on the tarmac and walked under the port wing.

"Good morning, commander," Mike said cheerfully. He had noted the pilot's ID tag on the left breast of his flight suit — LCDR JOHN MERRICK, USNR. "How's the weather enroute to Fallon?"

"Not bad this early in the morning." LCDR Merrick moved out from under the wheel well. "A lot of thunderbumpers along the Sierras later in the day."

"We had a rough one coming in from Phoenix last night."

"So I heard. It's been bad that direction most of the week. I fly for PSA, out of San Diego and I've made the Phoenix run several times the last few days."

"I'm with Air Arizona outa Phoenix," Mike said.

"Ah, the silver and turquoise Convairs. I see you guys a lot. You a captain, Lieutenant...ah...?"

"Murphy. Mike Murphy. I was the chief pilot...until recently. I'm the director of operations now. I used to be both, but with our recent expansion I had to give up the chief pilot position. I pretty much fly a desk now. About the only air time I get is with the reserves."

"You guys are really growing, Mike. You must make pretty good money."

"Can't complain. I'm also a part owner. We've been damn lucky so far. We started with one surplus C-45 a little over three years ago."

"So I understand. Keep growing and you'll be our major competition on the west coast."

"Not really. We just fill in between the areas you don't serve. I don't think we'll become much larger. The market`s just not there. By the way, commander, did they get the fuel leak in this bird fixed? Last night it was pretty bad."

"Yeah. I saw the gripe on the yellow sheet. It was written off as no fuel leak detected. These old R-5's leak like a sieve. I've never flown one that didn't smell like a gas station."

"Nice talking to you, commander. Guess I had better get in line and let you complete your pre-flight." Mike retrieved his bag and joined the short line boarding the aircraft.

LTJG Mike Murphy reached down to his left and placed the master armament switch on and selected rockets. The F9F-6 Cougar jet ahead of him rocked its wings and broke smartly left and down. Mike started the elapsed time clock on his instrument panel. Through his earphones he heard, "Cougar-three's in on target...weapons hot."

Mike could see over his left shoulder the jet fighter diving toward the target on the desert floor. The bulls-eye was an old navy bus. Ten seconds elapsed. Mike rocked his wings and slapped the control stick against his left knee. The Cougar responded instantly with a left roll. "Cougar-four's in on target...weapons hot," Mike reported. It was his eighth and final rocket run.

Pushing the stick forward, Mike entered a steep diving turn toward the bus.

"Cougar-three's off target...weapons cold," crackled through Mike's earphones.

Mike snapped his wings level on a heading of 090 degrees. He eased the nose lower, placing the target bus in the lighted cross-hairs of his gun sight. With the bus steady in the cross-hairs, he squeezed the trigger on the control stick firing a SCAR rocket from the starboard wing station. He monitored the rocket's trajectory by the white smoke trailing behind it. It appeared to be headed directly for the bulls-eye. Mike pulled sharply up off target and safed his Armament switch. "Cougar-four's off target...weapons cold," he called. "Roger, four. Your last rocket a bulls-eye," replied the ground spotter located in a tower 300 yards from the impact area.

"Cougar flight, this is Cougar-lead. Check for hung ordnance and safe all weapons. Rendezvous over target at angels twelve point five."

"Roger," was the response from the three other pilots in the flight. Mike was the last airplane off the target and had the greatest distance to cover to join the flight. He pushed the throttle full forward and began a steep climbing left turn. He spotted the lead aircraft and the other two in the process of joining on the leader. They were in a left turn about 2,000 feet above him.

"Two's in," reported the second aircraft in the flight as he moved into a position slightly behind and to the left of the leader.

The third aircraft joined on Cougar-two's left wing. When stabilized, Cougar-three dipped under the second aircraft and took a position on the lead's right wing forming a *V*. "Three's in."

Mike drifted into a position on Cougar-two's left wing easing the throttle back to match the formation's speed. When the relative motion ceased, Mike dipped under the formation and came up on Cougar-three's right wing. The aircraft were now in parade formation —the basic formation for operating a flight of four aircraft. "Four's in," he called.

"Roger, Cougar flight, this is lead. Anyone have a low fuel state?"

Each of the pilots in formation responded with, "Negative."

"Okay, then...let's have some fun. Cougar flight go to free cruise. Follow the leader."

The three trailing aircraft moved to a position in line with the leader and slightly below the aircraft ahead. The separation of the aircraft nose to tail was fifteen to twenty feet. In free cruise each pilot maintained his position by watching the tail of the aircraft ahead and keeping a constant distance.

Mike adjusted power and made control inputs to keep the aircraft ahead of him in the same relative position. He caught a glimpse of the desert and mountain horizon rotating in a clockwise direction and realized the flight was making a left aileron roll. When the horizon returned to normal it began moving upward as the flight entered a steep dive.

"Cougar flight, Cougar-lead. Anyone have problems with the roll?"

Again, each pilot responded with a, "Negative."

"Okay then, let's go up and over."

Mike felt the G's pushing him down in the seat as the flight transitioned from a dive into a steep climb. The horizon dropped from view as Mike added additional power to maintain his position. He could now see the horizon coming into view again above the Cougar in front of him. They were over the top of a loop and diving earthward.

"Cougar flight, Cougar-lead...let's hit the deck."

Mike retarded his throttle as gravity added to the velocity of the dive. He could see his altimeter unwinding rapidly as the airspeed indicator crept toward 600 knots.

The leader leveled at about two hundred feet above the barren desert floor. Mike's radar altimeter rose and fell from fifty to two hundred feet as the flight flashed across the terrain southeast of the air station. The lead aircraft dodged left and right avoiding small sand hills. From the number four position, Mike could see that his aircraft was below the protrusions. Fun is fun, he thought...but this was getting a little hairy. Visions of similar terrain in southeastern California flashed through his mind. One similar pile of sand had destroyed his jet aircraft and nearly cost him his life, not to mention his budding naval career.

"Cougar flight, Cougar-lead...let's take it up to angels six and I'll call for landing."

As they leveled at six thousand feet above sea level — about two thousand feet above the ground — Mike could sense the tension in his body and feel the moisture of his sweat-soaked flight suit. It was exhilarating. God, this was great, right where he belonged...in the air, not behind some cluttered desk waiting for the next surprise from Doris Dushane Kissling.

"Navy Fallon, this is Cougar flight leader with three chicks, ten miles south for landing...over."

"Roger, Cougar leader. You're cleared straight in to Runway 31. Altimeter is 29.92. Call your break."

"Roger, Fallon...call the break. Cougar flight go right echelon now."

The three tailing aircraft moved to the right of the leader and took positions slightly below each other. Mike could see the air station ahead on the horizon. The flight descended to five thousand feet and aligned with Runway 31.

AIR ARIZONA

Crossing the approach end of the runway, Cougar-lead called the break, "Fallon tower, Cougar flight at the break for 31." He rocked his wings and banked sharply to the left to enter the downwind leg of the traffic pattern.

Five seconds later, Cougar-two broke, and five seconds more, Cougar-three. Mike counted the seconds to himself and on five, banked sharply left reducing his power and dropping the speed brakes. The aircraft slowed rapidly. At 220 knots, Mike lowered the landing gear and retracted the speed brakes. He rolled level on a heading of 130 degrees and lowered his wing flaps. At 140 knots he added power to maintain that speed. Abeam the approach end of the runway he entered a 25 degree left bank and began a power-on rate of descent of about 600 feet per minute with 20 units angle of attack. The aircraft settled to the runway approximately 500 feet behind Cougar-three.

Lieutenant Commander Steel, the squadron operations officer and leader of the Cougar flight, waited for the three other pilots to complete the post-flight maintenance reports. When finished he gathered the pilots around him. "Good flight. I'm proud of you. We had a total of seven bulls-eyes. Mike, had three of them. Good shooting. Any problems with the free cruise maneuvers?"

The three shook their heads, indicating no.

"How about the low level? How was it back in the four position, Mike?"

"A little hairy, commander...but fun. I was scooping up sand with the jet intakes."

"I'll keep it a little higher next time. By the way, we launch again at thirteen hundred. We'll be on the West Range for some air-to-air gunnery with a towed sleeve target. Get some lunch and be ready to go at twelve-thirty."

AIR ARIZONA

CHAPTER 17

At exactly 1300, Cougar-lead began his takeoff roll on Runway 31. Cougar-two began rolling five seconds later followed by Cougar-three in another five seconds. Mike Murphy began his count—thousand one...thousand two...thousand three. At five he shoved the throttle forward to 100 percent power output. The F9F-6 began rolling forward, slowly at first, but gained speed rapidly. At 124 knots indicated airspeed Mike eased the stick back and the nosewheel lifted off the runway. A moment later the main gear broke free of the concrete and the Cougar vaulted skyward. Clearing the end of the runway, Mike raised the landing gear and rolled the craft left in a steep climbing turn to join the other three aircraft on a westerly heading.

"Cougar flight, this is Cougar-lead. Radio check on tac-channel three...over."

"Cougar-lead, Cougar-two is in your seven o'clock closing. Read you loud and clear."

"Cougar-lead, Cougar-three is in your eight o'clock closing. Loud an clear."

Mike keyed his UHF transceiver. "Cougar-lead, Cougar-four. I have you in sight...be with you in about a minute. Read you loud and clear."

"Roger Cougar flight. All chicks loud and clear. Remain this frequency. Break. Jackstay Niner-six, Cougar flight is inbound to the

West Range for air-to-air. Say your position."

"Cougar-lead, Jackstay niner-six is at the southwest corner of the West Range, angels 15 on a heading of 040 degrees. We'll be streaming the bucket shortly. Commence your live runs from my port side. The bucket will be approximately five thousand feet behind us."

Mike eased his Cougar into a left echelon formation in the number four spot. Ahead of the flight he could see Jackstay 96, a Navy JD-1 twin-engine propeller driven aircraft. The JD-1 was the Navy's version of the Air Force A-26 Invader.

Cougar-lead began a gentle right turn to align the flight on the left side of Jackstay 96. The flight positioned itself about five thousand feet off the left wingtip of the target towing aircraft so that firing runs at the target, about a mile behind the tow plane, would be in a direction away from Jackstay 96. The target, called a bucket, was a white canvas windsock attached to the tow plane by a steel wire cable. The tow aircraft had the capability of instantly releasing the target in an emergency.

Each Cougar aircraft in the flight had twenty millimeter shells with the projectile's nose painted a different color from the ammunition in the other three jets. Projectiles hitting the bucket left smudges of their color on the canvas and allowed the scoring of hits by each aircraft. When the mission was complete the tow plane would reel in the cable until the target was approximately 100 feet behind. The tow plane would then fly alongside the runway at 200 feet above the surface and cut the cable, allowing the target to fall to the ground. The bucket would be retrieved by ground crewmen who would tally the score for each aircraft.

Occasionally, a stray or poorly aimed projectile would hit the tow aircraft which would abruptly halt the mission. One tow aircraft had actually crashed last year during training after several twenty millimeter projectiles tore through the cockpit killing the pilot.

"Jackstay niner-six, Cougar-lead. We're ready to commence live runs."

"Roger, Cougar-lead. Cleared to commence live runs."

Cougar-lead rocked his wings and broke sharply right. "Cougar-lead is in...weapons hot."

Mike checked the armament switch in the cockpit insuring it was in the *guns* position. He would leave the Master switch off until he made his turn into the target and the nose had cleared the tow aircraft.

Completing their runs from the port side, the aircraft would then join in a right echelon on the right side of the tow aircraft and make their next runs from starboard. This routine continued until the tow aircraft approached the limits of the military restricted area where it would make a 180 degree turn back into the gunnery range.

Following Cougar-three's off cold report, Mike banked sharply toward the target and armed his guns. He concentrated on putting the bucket in the cross-hairs of his gun sight and keeping it there. As he closed the target he placed his right index finger on the trigger switch on the control stick. At a distance of about one thousand feet from the bucket, he squeezed the trigger and watched the tracers stream toward the canvas target. He cautioned himself not to fixate on the target and fly into it. Target fixation and the desire to get hits on air targets or ground targets killed several pilots each year. They simply flew into the target before breaking off their runs.

Mike released the trigger and adjusted his heading to pass behind the target. Once by, he turned toward the three other aircraft to join up for another run.

Mike set up for his next pass. One by one, the Cougar jets peeled off to the left making firing runs. Following Cougar-three's off cold report, Mike slapped the stick to his left thigh and felt the force of the sharp turn pin him to his seat. Satisfied he was locked on target he squeezed off a burst of cannon fire which appeared to stream directly into the bucket. He was elated. This was what he wanted out of life. Thrills. Excitement. He was a fighter pilot through and through...not a desk jockey. To hell with Air Arizona. To hell with director of operations. To hell with Doris Dushane Kissling. This was his element...where he belonged. He snapped the Cougar jet back to the right to join the formation. It was his best run so far. The next would be even better. So what if he was the junior pilot by rank in the squadron, passed over initially for LTJG, released from active duty at the earliest possible date. So what. He was a damn good pilot, and he would show his superiors this day that he was a top gun fighter pilot.

"Cougar-four's off...weapons cold." Mike slid into formation beside Cougar-three.

"Cougar flight, Cougar-lead. I believe we can squeeze one more run in before we run outa range. Cougar-lead is in...weapons hot."

Mike relaxed and took a deep breath. The adrenaline flow on his last run had been high. He was pumped and ready to go again. A quick glance at his instruments revealed a high tailpipe temperature, nearly 800 degrees—well over the normal temperature of 540 degrees. "Cougar-lead, Cougar-four. I'm indicating a high TPT."

"Roger, four. What is it?"

"It's well above the red line, nearly eight hundred."

"Roger, four. Recommend you return to base. Do you want an escort?"

"That's negative. I'll reduce power and return to Fallon. I'll set up for a flame-out approach, just in case. You guys go ahead and have some fun. I'll see you back on the deck." Mike reduced engine power and turned right. The TPT dropped to 720 degrees. He aligned the course bar in his VOR receiver which was tuned to the air base VORTAC transmitter. The needle indicated a course of 105 degrees magnetic to the field. He steadied on course and called the control tower. "Navy Fallon tower, Cougar-four's thirty miles west requesting a precautionary flame-out approach and landing."

"Roger, Cougar-four. Say reason for request."

"Tower, I have a high TPT indication. Everything else looks good. Probably a faulty indicator."

"Roger, Cougar-four. Call high key and we'll close the field to other traffic until you're on the runway."

Mike began to mentally plan his approach. Seven thousand feet above the ground at initial point, airspeed 210 knots, gear and flaps down. The tailpipe temperature gauge suddenly pegged out. "Navy Fallon tower, Cougar-four. The TPT is pegged. I'm declaring an emergency now."

"Roger, Cougar-four. Break. All aircraft in the Fallon area, the airfield is closed for an emergency. I say again, the airfield is closed. We have a Cougar inbound from the west with an emergency."

A red light on the instrument panel illuminated indicating a generator failure. "Navy Fallon, Cougar-four. I have a—"
Another red light came on indicating loss of fuel pressure. "I have two warning—" Two more lights lit, indicating a fire. "I have four red warning lights on now. I think I just won a free game." A fifth warning light illuminated. The aircraft began to buffet wildly. Mike could feel the fire at his back. Turning his head to the right he saw flames shooting through the fuselage. The plane would explode any second. He positioned himself upright in the seat, his head pushed back against the headrest. He slid his feet off the rudder pedals and put them beneath the seat. There was no time to transmit his intentions. With both hands, he reached above his head grabbing the ejection seat face cover. He pulled forward hard, firing the seat through the Plexiglas canopy. He went up...up...up. At the top of the ejection arc the pressure ceased. He released the face curtain to see the jet below and ahead of him burst into a ball of fire. Pieces scattered in all directions, most leaving a trail of smoke behind. The largest piece, the cockpit and part of the right wing spiraled downward. He had no sensation of falling. He was simply suspended in space watching the fragmented remains of his F9F-6 Cougar plummet earthward. He reached for the seatbelt release handle and gave it a tug. It didn't open. Another tug. The handle was jammed. Still no sensation of falling, but objects on the ground were growing larger. He observed what appeared to be a small community, nothing more than eight or ten mobile homes arranged in a circle. A dirt road from the trailer compound extended northward. Dry washes and sage brush were the only other objects below him.

Mike grasped the seatbelt with his left hand and with his right, tugged fiercely at the release handle. It snapped open. He reached for the D-ring on the parachute harness to release the chute from its pack, but suddenly realized he had not separated from the ejection seat. He pushed the seat downward with both hands causing it to separate a short distance from his body. With both feet he kicked the seat with all his strength and it tumbled away from him. Now he sensed he was falling—objects on the ground grew larger. The ground rushed rapidly toward him. He grasped the harness with his left hand, and with his right, gave the D-ring a hard pull separating it from its pocket.

Article in the *Fallon Eagle Standard Newspaper*, dated August 5, 1960:

NAVY FLIER MISSING

A Navy Reserve pilot flying a gunnery mission on the gunnery range west of the air station yesterday reported an emergency with his craft. The control tower lost communications with the pilot shortly after he reported the malfunction. The remains of the F9F-6 Cougar jet were discovered approximately 30 miles west of the air station scattered over several square miles. The ejection seat or remains of the pilot were not located. The only habitation near the accident site is the Wild Horse Ranch, a bordello consisting of a number of mobile homes located in a sparse region of Storey County. Inquiries at the ranch revealed the residents heard a loud explosion but did not see a parachute nor the pilot. The identity of the pilot has not been released by navy officials at the base.

Article in the August 6 edition of the *Arizona Republic*:

LOCAL RESERVE PILOT MISSING IN TRAINING CRASH

AIR ARIZONA

The Navy identified the pilot of a F9F-6 Cougar jet aircraft which crashed last Thursday at the Fallon, Nevada naval gunnery range east of Reno. The pilot was identified as Lieutenant Junior Grade Michael M. Murphy of Phoenix. Mr. Murphy is employed by Air Arizona as director of operations. Mr. Murphy has no living next of kin. Doris Kissling, President of Air Arizona, had no comment.

A spokesman at the Fallon Naval Air Station said the search for the missing pilot would continue.

Article from the August 8 edition of the *Arizona Republic*:

MISSING RESERVE PILOT FOUND

Lieutenant Junior Grade Michael M. Murphy, missing since the crash of his navy jet fighter last Thursday, has been found safe and sound. Authorities from the Fallon, Nevada, Naval Auxiliary Air Station reported that the missing pilot called the air station from the Wild Horse Ranch, a legal bordello located west of the airfield. He told authorities that he had suffered amnesia shortly after ejecting from his disabled jet. His parachute landed in the center of the bordello which is a circle of ten single-wide mobile homes. He didn't know who or where he was, but residents of the ranch promised to help him. Sunday evening he suddenly regained his senses and called the air station.

Authorities are at a loss to explain why the proprietor reported that she had not seen the downed pilot. Doctors at the air station examined Murphy and found no injuries or medical problems except extreme exhaustion. After several days of bed rest, the pilot should be able to resume his flight duties.

When notified by telephone that Mr. Murphy had been located at the bordello, Doris Kissling, President of Air Arizona where the pilot is employed, made no comment. She simply laughed and hung up.

CHAPTER 18

"Come on, Mike...damnit! Tell me the truth. Did you or didn't you have amnesia?" Tad Little place his half-full coffee cup on the director of operations' desk. "Quit bullshitting me."

A sly smile crept across Mike Murphy's face. "Of course I had amnesia, Tad. You don't think I'd lie around a whorehouse for three whole days while half the navy and law enforcement personnel in the area searched for me, do you? Not even I could do that, good buddy."

"Good buddy, bullshit. I know you, Mike. You're lying your ass off. You were messing with the gals, weren't you?"

"Sorry, Tad. You can quit fantasizing. I was really out of it for three days. I didn't know where I was or who I was."

"Sure...and what did the girls do for three days, just look at you?"

Mike offered a broader smile. "No. They nursed me back to good health. Some long hot baths and massages. They really cared for me."

"Mike, you're lying through your teeth." Tad retrieved his cup from Mike's desk and started for the door. "By the way, Doris wants to see you. Just give her a call."

"At the bank?"

"No...at her home. She wants you to drop by. She's got another wild-ass idea." Tad left the office, slamming the door on his way out.

Mike swung the red Corvette left off Scottsdale Road onto Hummingbird Lane. As he approached the steep upgrade, he shoved the gear lever from third to second, gunning the engine between gears. He loved the deep lion-like roar the V-8 engine produced when coaxed with the throttle. As he passed Quartz Mountain Road, he slowed and shifted to first gear with another tap of the throttle, then turned right into a private drive. He brought the Corvette to a stop just short of a closed large wrought iron gate where he put the transmission in neutral leaving the engine at a deep-throated idle.

What kind of wild hair does she have up her butt this time, he wondered. He reached over with his left hand and pushed the button on a speaker box mounted on a black iron pole next to the Corvette.

"Yes," a male voice boomed from the speaker.

"It's Mike Murphy...to see Mrs. Kissling. She's expecting me."

"Just a moment, sir," the speaker box answered.

Mike surveyed the area beyond the large white pueblo-style stucco mansion. He could see twenty, maybe thirty miles across the desert floor north of Scottsdale. As youngsters, he and Tad had hunted quail and dove in the area. Coyote, fox and javelina pig also roamed the region then, but not now. Scottsdale and the Paradise Valley areas were bursting at their seams as they sprawled northward. Housing developments and shopping centers sprung up like wild flowers.

There was a buzz from the speaker and the large gate swung inward. Mike drove forward and parked in front of the mammoth three-level home of Doris Kissling. *Just how much fuckin' money does she have*? he wondered. He started to lock the doors of the Corvette when he remembered he was in a five acre fenced compound with a guard on full-time duty. He had been to the home only twice before, for Christmas parties, and he hadn't liked the guests Doris had invited. He felt out of place rubbing elbows with multi-millionaires. They never flew with Air Arizona Airlines. They had their own corporate or private planes.

He walked to the large double-doors and pressed the door bell. Musical chimes inside responded.

The door opened and Mike was greeted by a large Mexican

woman. "*Meester* Murphy, *entrada por favor. Buenos dias. Meeses Keesling ees* expecting you. *Shee'es* by the pool. Come *theese* way, *por favor*."

Mike followed the broad-beamed servant through the entry hall into the living room. Quick side glances assured Mike that whatever amount of money Doris Kissling had, it was more than enough. Large original oil paintings adorned the stucco walls and numerous sculptures sat on tables or stood in corners. The white carpet was so deep-piled that it was difficult to walk without a conscious effort to raise the feet higher.

The maid stopped at a large sliding glass door. She pointed to the enormous swimming pool and patio outside. "*Meeses Keesling esta para alla*."

Mike slid open the door and walked toward the pool. He did not see Doris. Suddenly she appeared, popping up from a lounge chair with its back toward Mike. She wore a small blue bikini bottom and nothing else. She had a blue halter in her hand having obviously been sunning herself.

"Here, Mike," she said handing him the halter. "I tried to get this damned thing on when you opened the door, but I couldn't reach far enough behind me to fasten it. Be a good boy and fasten it for me." She turned her back showing no sign of embarrassment over the incident.

I wonder how she gets it on when no one is around, Mike pondered, not really accepting that she couldn't fasten it herself. The freckles on her back reminded Mike that thirteen years ago she also had freckles on her face—all over her body, for that matter. They had skinny-dipped together one hot afternoon in the Verde River near Bartlett Dam. With no one around, Mike had removed the seat from his 1936 Ford coupe and placed it on the ground near the river. They had engaged in passionate love-making for several hours. For Mike it was only the third time he had experienced physical love. The first two times occurred in a drive-in theater with Mary Maroni. She was a slim brunette with very little meat on her bones—especially the pubic bone. The boys called her *Bony Maroni*. Trying to maneuver around the steering wheel and stick gearshift on the floor and pounding against the hard bone was a painful experience for Mike. He was sore for several days, hardly able to wear his tight-fitting jockey undershorts. He wondered what was so great about sex that all the boys talked about in gym class. Doris had cleared up that mystery for him. She was totally uninhibited when it came to sex. She showed and taught him things that he had only dreamed about, and that other boys talked about but never experienced.

His loins stirred, his hands shook as he connected the two ends of the halter behind her back. He wanted to spin her around and shout, *Let's go back, Doris. Back to the days by the river...back to the warm evenings in Encanto Park where we waded out to an island in the lagoon and made love for hours...back to the days when we parked by the large rock formation known as the ship and squirmed and wiggled in the front seat of the old Ford until I cried out, "No more...no more...I can't no more...I'm exhausted."*

Doris turned and faced him. "You wanted to say something, Mike?"

Mike stared at the woman before him, at her dark auburn hair that once had been blazing red, at the smooth un-freckled face with the high cheekbones, at the deep green pools that were her eyes, at the sheer confidence she exuded. This was not the *days by the river Doris*, not the *Encanto Park Doris* or the *ship Doris*...this was Mrs. Doris Dushane Kissling, the very wealthy and shrewd president of Air Arizona Airlines who, with no more than a snap of her fingers and several thousand dollars, could put him out on the street unemployed. "No, Doris, I wasn't about to say anything. What was it you wanted to talk about?"

"Did Tad tell you what I had in mind?"

"No, he just said you had another wild...I mean, another new idea."

"Have a seat, Mike." Doris pointed to a lounge chair next to hers. "I'll have Juanita bring us a drink. Beefeater martini on the rocks with three olives, if I remember correctly."

Mike nodded his head and sat in the chair beside Doris.

Doris pushed the button on the speaker box next to her chair. "Juanita."

A short pause, then, "*Si, senora.*"

"Please bring Mr. Murphy a gin martini with three olives. I'll have my usual."

Doris turned to Mike. "Ever hear of Big Sky Airlines?"

"Out of Montana? Run three or four airplanes up and down the Rockies?"

"Out of Billings, Montana, Mike. They have six Convair 340's." Doris paused. "We're going to buy them out, lock, stock and barrel."

Mike's jaw dropped. He started to speak—but couldn't.

Doris pushed the speaker button again. "Juanita, better make Mr. Murphy's martini a double."

AIR ARIZONA

CHAPTER 19

True to her word, Doris Kissling, negotiating as president of Air Arizona Airlines, purchased Big Sky Airlines—*lock, stock and barrel*—including six Convair 340's, hangar, office and maintenance facilities at the Billings Logan International Airport, slot times and landing rights at Casper, Denver, Salt Lake City, Pocatello and Missoula. All but a few of the Big Sky Airlines employees, including twenty-four pilots, relocated to Phoenix to become a part of Air Arizona Airlines, now the largest regional airlines in the West.

With a shrug of the shoulders and a grunt, Buck Skin accepted the position of station manager at the Billings' facilities. Eight maintenance personnel and four ticket agents remained in Billings to work for the new manager.

Mike flipped the lever on the intercom box on his desk. "Judy, get in here right now...pronto."

Five seconds later Mike's office door swung open. Six feet four inches of broad shoulders and lean muscle walked in. "What is it now, Mike?"

"Judy...goddamnit! Where'd you get a name like Judy? Judy George? Your parents must have hated you to name you Judy."

"They wanted a girl, I guess. There were already four boys in the family—Robert, James, Earl and Joseph. I guess they thought if they gave me a girl's name before I was born, they'd get a girl. I turned out

108

to be the runt in the family."

"You must have had a hell of a time in school with a girl's name. A lot of kidding and stuff."

Judy eased his towering body into a chair in front of Mike's desk. "Not really. I was always the biggest guy in class, and I beat the crap outa anyone who teased me about my name. They just called me Jude after that. My friends all call me Jude."

"Okay, Jude it is." Mike picked up a sheet of paper from his desk. "You were operations manager at Big Sky...correct?"

"Correct. Now I guess I'm the assistant operations manager of Air Arizona. Correct?"

"Okay, assistant operations manager is fine with me, but your main job is scheduling our aircraft and crews."

"That's what I've been doing the three weeks I've been here. Is there a problem with next month's schedule?"

"Damn right there is, Jude. You've got three-six scheduled past the fifth. The bird goes to Aerodyne for overhaul and preventative maintenance on the fifth. That leaves us with no back-up bird. Also you've got Captain King burnt out of hours on the 25th...in Billings. That means we'll have send another captain up there and deadhead *Sky* King back. I don't know how you guys managed to run an airline with scheduling that screwed up. What'd you do if a plane needed maintenance and there was no back-up...or you ran a crew outa crew duty time away from home?"

"Hell, we'd just cancel the flight and tell the passengers they would have to wait till the next scheduled flight. It never was a big problem."

"Well maybe the cowboys and goat ropers up there in Montana didn't give a damn, but we've got a lot of business fliers here in the civilized part of the country that do give a damn. Cause one of them to miss or be late to a meeting and they'll find another airlines to fly. We don't cancel flights here. We don't even delay them unless there's one hell of a good reason."

"Well, Mike, to tell you the truth, we can't make the schedule we have now with the aircraft we've got. Ain't no way. I told Mrs. Kissling last night that we'll need—"

"Mrs. Kissling? What the hell were you doing talking to her?" Mike pounded his fist on the desk. "I talk to Mrs. Kissling. You talk to me. That's the way it works."

"She invited me and the wife to her house last night for cocktails and dinner. She wanted to get to know us. That's a real nice place she has up there, Mike. You ever been?"

Mike cupped his hands over his head and pushed down hard. "One...two...three." He regained his composure. "Yes, Judy...Jude. I've been up on the hill many times," he lied. "Now just what the hell did you tell the president? Did you tell her we'd just cancel flights when we ran outa planes and crews?"

"Of course not. I just told her we needed some more planes and crews, or we needed to cut back on our schedule."

"What'd Mrs. Kissling say when you told her that?"

"She just smiled and said she would take care of it. Not for me to worry."

"You're not a personal friend of Mrs. Kissling, are you, Jude? Usually when we get this screwed up around here it's because of one of her friends."

The intercom buzzed. "Mr. Murphy, Mrs. Kissling's on line two for you."

"Tell her I'll call back in a few minutes."

"Sir, she says she wants to talk to you right now."

Mike snapped up the telephone from his desk. "Yes?" he shouted.

"Mike...Mike...calm down. Things not going well today?"

"Not really smooth, you might say. What can I do for you?"

"Good news, Mike. Regis has negotiated another stop on the Billings run. Spokane, Washington. He should finish up the paperwork next week, and we can start service on the first of March."

"Doris, we haven't got enough airplanes or crews to service Spokane. We can't even make our present schedule work."

"I know, Mike. Didn't Jude tell you I've got that worked out?"

110

"Not exactly."

"We've got three more Convairs coming next week. You'll need to advance some of our first pilots to captain and hire some more copilots. Better get busy on that right now."

"Goddamnit, Doris! I'm not only the director of operations for this outfit, I'm part owner. I'd like to be cut in on some of this wheeling and dealing you and old Reggie-Boy are doing. That makes twenty-five aircraft we'll own. I'm not really sure we're ready for that right now. We've been flying with some empty seats lately. I think—"

"I am sure, Mike...damn sure. I've projected everything out. We'll be fine. We're less than half the size I want to be in five years. By then we'll have jets and be covering half the United States...maybe even Hawaii. If you don't want to be a part of this, just let me know. You know the deal?"

"I didn't say I wanted out, Doris. I just think we should be a little more conservative. Get all this equipment and the economy goes bad, we'll be on our ass."

"Mike, have I been wrong yet? I damn well know what I'm doing. Relax a little. Take some time off. Go down to Guaymas and do some fishing...or whatever you do down there. Take your little blue navy jet out and blow down some cacti and sagebrush. Jude can handle things while you're gone."

"Does Tad know about these new birds, Doris? I mean if he—"

"He knows, Mike. We talked about it last week. Relax. Come up and have a cool drink with me sometime. The pool's heated. Maybe I will be too."

Mike slammed down the phone. "Shit!"

Judy George stood up from his chair. A broad grin was on his face. "Anything else for me, boss?"

"No, Jude. I'm sorry I blew my top." Mike reached across the desk with his right hand. "Welcome to Air Arizona. When Doris Dushane Kissling says *shit*, everybody squats. Can you handle the office for a few days? I think I will call a couple of old friends in Hollywood and go fishing for a few days."

"Well, Mike, I'm just an old goat roper from Montana, but I think I can handle things for awhile. Go have yourself some fun. Doris...I mean Mrs. Kissling said you're one of those hot navy jet pilots with the reserves. I'd sure like to fly one of those stovepipes sometime."

Mike sat back down. "Sure, Jude, we've got a lot of goat ropers flying jets in the navy. One more sure wouldn't hurt."

Judy left the office, the wide shit-eating grin still across his face. Mike punched a button on his intercom. "Maintenance, this is Mr. Murphy. Will you please inform Mr. Little I need him in my office...right now?"

Mike flipped through the pile of papers on his desk. "Bullshit! This is bullshit too, and this one, and this one." He tossed them in the wastebasket.

The door opened and a frenzied Tad Little burst in. "What'd you need, Mike? We're working our butts off down there trying to get the Big Sky logos off two more aircraft."

"Sit down, Tad. How about a drink?" Mike reached down to the bottom drawer of his desk. "Got some Jose Cuervo in here. The gold stuff."

"Christ, not now, Mike. It's the middle of the morning. Besides, I'm trying to give that stuff up."

"Tad, did you know about the three new birds we're getting?" Mike retrieved a bottle of Beefeaters from the desk drawer and poured four to five ounces in his coffee cup.

"I knew, Mike. I knew last week. I wanted to tell you but Doris said not to bother you with it. Hey, Mike, you shouldn't be drinking that stuff here in your office...not during work hours."

"Well, Tad, good buddy, I'm on vacation as of five minutes ago. You got a new assistant down there too...from Big Sky?" Mike drained the contents of the cup. "Not bad with a little cold coffee. I think I just came up with a new cocktail—coffeetini."

"I've got a Mr. Buttons from Big Sky working with me, Mike. He's damn good. Knows the Convair inside and out."

"What's his first name, Tad...this new goat roper assistant?"

"Theodore...but everyone calls him Punch. You know, *punch buttons*."

"I knew it, goddamnit! I knew it. Doris has bought a fuckin' Punch and Judy airlines from Montana to merge with us. We're a goddamned puppet show airlines." Mike took the Beefeater bottle and poured several more ounces in his cup. "Tell old Punch you're taking four or five days off and that he's got it. We're going down to Guaymas for a great fuckin' adventure. Call Buzz and see if he's got a Cessna one-eighty we can use for a few days. If not, call Sawyer Aviation and get us a Cessna—any model. All you do is add five miles an hour for each model you go up. Shit! I know that. I'll give Dolores and Bobbi a call."

CHAPTER 20

Doris Kissling took a drink of water from a glass on the table before her, cleared her throat and stood. "Gentlemen, the seventh annual meeting of the Air Arizona stockholders is now in session. Mr. Rothchild, please enter in the minutes the date, April 3rd, 1965, and those in attendance—myself, Mr. Michael Murphy, director of operations, and Mr. Thadeus Little, director of maintenance. Once again, Mr. Rothchild is serving as recorder and legal advisor."

Doris took her seat and shuffled through the large stack of papers before her. "We have a lot of business to conduct today, but before I start, I believe congratulations are in order for Mr. Murphy who has recently been promoted to lieutenant commander in the naval reserve. Is that right, Mike?"

Mike Murphy nodded his head. Regis Rothchild scribbled on a yellow legal pad in front of him.

"First on the agenda, gentlemen, is the opportunity for a merger." Doris paused and stared at Mike. "Yes, Mike?"

"I didn't say anything," Mike answered.

"Somehow I feel you were about to. Go ahead."

"I'll wait." Mike poured a glass of water and took a sip.

"Regis and I have been negotiating with Cal-West and it appears that we have reached an agreement to merge. As you know, Cal-West operates a fleet of twenty aircraft out of Los Angeles to twelve cities in California, Oregon and Washington. The biggest sticking point in the negotiations was whether we could retain the Air Arizona name. We won that one."

"Mrs. Kissling, excuse me," Tad Little said. "If I'm not mistaken, Cal-West has a fleet of F-27 Friendships."

"You're not mistaken, Tad. They do fly F-27's."

"That's gonna make one hell of a maintenance nightmare, trying to operate and maintain two different kinds of airplanes. The F-27's have jet turbo-prop engines. That's a whole new ball game compared to the R-2800 reciprocating engines the Convairs have. There are damned few mechanics that can work on both types." Tad turned to Mike Murphy.

Mike nodded his head in agreement but did not speak.

"If that's your only worry, Tad, forget it. We will not be operating two types of aircraft...just the turbo-props. Cal-West has twenty more on order from the Netherlands, but poor financial management has put them on the brink of bankruptcy. A merger with us will pull them out of a hole and put Air Arizona into the jet age."

"What about the Convairs?" Tad asked. "They've been our bread and butter."

"We're through with bread and butter, Tad. It's time for a little caviar and champagne. We'll dump the Convairs. There's a good market for them now in South America."

"But that's like starting all over again, Doris. I mean...shit! Excuse me. We'll have to get rid of some of our people, retrain others, hire new ones. What'd you think, Mike?"

"Sounds good to me, Tad." Mike took a long drink of water.

Doris looked at Mike with amazement. "You agree, Mike?"

"Sure...it's about time we tried something new. We haven't bought any new planes or airlines in almost five years."

"Mike, you're kidding...aren't you?" Tad asked. "You go along with this merger?"

Mike nodded again.

Regis Rothchild looked up from his writing at Mike. He appeared also to be stunned by Mike's response.

Doris continued. "We'll have a good nucleus of trained pilots and mechanics from Cal-West. Mike, you and Tad will need to prepare a plan to incorporate their personnel with ours. I want you to cull through our people and pick out the best. Let the others go. You'll have to hire some new people with jet experience. We'll phase in gradually. As each new F-27 is received, we'll get rid of a Convair. That means for a period of nearly six months we'll be operating both types. You two will retain your positions as directors of operations and maintenance. With this size organization we'll need a third department to handle financial matters. The CEO of Cal-West will be our new comptroller and will head the Financial Department."

"I thought they just went broke with poor money management," Tad interrupted.

"I believe under my supervision he will do more than an adequate job for us."

"Oh!" Tad added.

"We have been fortunate to operate the eight years we have been in business with only three shareholders, and we have done well for ourselves."

More, some than others, Mike thought.

"However, Cal-West is a corporation with stock listed on the American Exchange...and Air Arizona Airlines will be incorporated as such. Mike, you and Tad will be issued shares that correspond to your interest in our present company. A goodly share, I might add. I will still own the controlling interest.

"Now, gentlemen, are there any questions?"

Tad offered a blank stare of disbelief. Mike fiddled with his glass of water wiping the condensation off the outside.

"I'm surprised, Mike," Doris said. "You usually are quite vocal on these matters...especially when we expand. Apparently you have come to trust my judgment."

"Believe me, Mrs. Kissling. I trust your judgment completely," Mike replied.

"Also, before we close, I have received some inside information from a trusted friend in Congress which might become a mint for us in the future. He said the build-up in Southeast Asia is going to accelerate rapidly, with thousands of more troops going there. He said that the Military Air Transport Service will be fully utilized hauling war supplies. Contracts will be offered to airlines for transporting troops. Very lucrative contracts, I might add. I'm not one to wish our country goes to all-out war, but wars have made many fortunes for those wise enough to take advantage of the situation. I have the option to lease five Douglas DC-8's, if we can snag one of these contracts.

"Now, before I close the meeting, is there any other business we need to conduct."

"Just one more thing, Doris." Mike sat up squarely in his chair.

"What's that, Mike?"

"I need a leave of absence...or something."

"A leave of absence? You mean like a vacation? A few weeks off?"

Tad turned a surprised face to look at his friend.

"Longer than that, Doris. Several months ago I received a letter from the Navy Bureau of Personnel encouraging reserve pilots to return to active duty. Looks like they must know about the build-up in Southeast Asia also. I applied. Yesterday I received orders to the Leemore Naval Air Station in California for refresher training and then to Attack Squadron 216 onboard the USS *Hancock*.

CHAPTER 21

As the flight of A-4C Skyhawks crossed the shore line headed seaward, Lieutenant Commander Mike Murphy keyed his lip microphone and transmitted. "Home Plate, this is Diamond eight-seven with a flight of four. Feet wet, inbound to you."

"Roger, Diamond eight-seven," answered an air controller onboard the USS *Hancock* operating on Yankee Station in the Gulf of Tonkin. "Contact Pri-Fly at five miles."

"Roger, Pri-Fly at five." Mike switched back to tactical frequency. "Diamond flight, Diamond-lead. Anyone with hung ordnance or damage?"

Each aircraft in the flight responded with a negative.

"Diamond-lead, this is two. Looks like you have some damage on your under-fuselage near the tail. I'll close up and take a better look."

"Roger, two."

The Skyhawk on Mike's left wing moved under the lead aircraft. "Diamond-lead, you have some damage aft near the tailpipe and around the hook area...also some hydraulic fluid streaks. Doesn't look too bad."

"Roger, two. Everything in the cockpit looks good. Diamond flight, let's tighten up the formation and take it down to angels two."

The three trailing Skyhawks closed into a tight parade formation and started a descent.

"Diamond flight, Diamond-lead...go button three now." The

118

TACAN indicator on Mike's instrument panel registered five miles.

"Pri-fly, Diamond eight-seven at five, a flight of four for recovery. Negative hung ordnance. Lead has some minor damage under the tail. Should be no problem for landing."

"Roger, Diamond eight-seven and flight. Your signal is *Charlie* upon arrival. Recovery course is 080 degrees with 31 knots of wind over the deck. Say your playmates' call signs."

"Roger, Pri-Fly. Understand *Charlie* upon arrival. Playmates are Diamonds zero-six, zero-one and niner-three." Mike turned the formation to a heading of 080 degrees magnetic to parallel the ship's course. "Diamond flight, Diamond-lead...right echelon now."

Diamond-two slid under the leader and took a position on the leader's right wing. All four Skyhawks were now stacked in a right echelon formation. They flew down the starboard side of the *Hancock* at an altitude of 800 feet. On clear days like this, the aircraft made normal carrier recoveries maintaining visual reference to the ship at all times. At night or in foul weather, the aircraft marshaled overhead the carrier and were directed to a landing, one by one, by radar controllers aboard ship.

"Diamond flight, Diamond-lead...hooks down now."

Each pilot in the flight positioned their tailhook lever to *Down*.

"Diamond-lead, this is two. A negative on your tailhook."

Mike checked the tailhook indicator in the cockpit. It indicated *Up*. "Roger, two. I'll try it again." He recycled the lever to *Up* and back to *Down*. Still no hook down indication.

"Pri-Fly, Diamond eight-seven. I have a negative hook down indication. Request to climb overhead to angels two and have my wingman check it out."

"Roger, Diamond eight-seven, you're cleared to angels two with Diamond zero-six. Break. Diamonds zero-one and niner-three, continue your approach."

Mike added power to the Skyhawk commencing a climb to 2000 feet. His wingman, Diamond 06, climbed with him.

"Diamond-lead, this is two. I'm gonna close up behind you and take a look."

"Roger, Two. I'll recycle again." Mike positioned the lever to *Up* and back to *Down*.

"Diamond-lead, this is two. I think I see the problem. Your hook is down a few inches but it looks like it's jammed by a piece of jagged metal. Must be where you took a hit."

"Roger, two. Thanks. Break. Pri-Fly, did you copy Diamond zero-six's report?"

"Affirmative, Diamond eight-seven. Hold overhead at angels two. Say your fuel state."

"Pri-Fly, Diamond eight-seven's good for about fifty-five minutes at cruise."

"Roger, Diamond eight-seven. Break. Diamond zero-six, you're cleared back to the break. Your signal is *Charlie*."

Mike eased back on the throttle to save fuel and commenced a gradual left turn orbit at 2000 feet over the *Hancock*. He observed each of the three Skyhawks in his flight make their arrested landings onboard the carrier. Also he could see the carrier deck being re-spotted for another launch.

"Diamond eight-seven, Pri-Fly. The air group commander advises bingo to Danang and have repairs made by the Marine Detachment. Advise Home Plate by message when ready to return. Contact Home Plate on button five for pigeons to Danang."

"Roger, Pri-Fly. Switching now." Mike added power and began a climb on a southerly heading. "Home Plate, this is Diamond eight-seven up your frequency. Request pigeons to Danang."

"Roger, Diamond eight-seven. Vector heading 115 degrees, 187 miles. Contact Danang Approach Control on 342.2 at twenty-five miles out."

"Roger, Home Plate. Heading 115 degrees, 187 miles. Request radar tracking until I have contact with Danang Approach."

Mike loosened his lap and shoulder harness. He kept it snug tightly for carrier landings and low altitude flying. Time to relax for a few minutes. It was about thirty-five minutes flying time to Danang.

He would be low on fuel when he arrived, but the weather along the coast was clear and he would call low fuel state when he contacted Danang Approach. That would give him priority over other non-emergency aircraft in the landing pattern. Mike fished through the large pouch-like pocket on the lower right leg of his flight suit and retrieved a package of Camels. He took a cigarette from the pack and returned the package to the pocket. He turned the oxygen flow off and detached his oxygen mask from the right side of his helmet. With a Zippo lighter from his left sleeve pocket, he lit the cigarette and took a deep drag. He had only time for a few deep inhalations before having to return the mask to his face and breath 100 percent oxygen. It had been a wild six months since the *Hancock* had arrived on Yankee Station. He had flown countless missions over North Vietnam and the waters of the Tonkin Gulf, bombed bridges and highways that were repaired in hours, bombed and fired rockets into suspected surface-to-air missile sites, sank two enemy patrol boats, strafed trucks and enemy troops winding their way down the infamous Ho Chi Minh Trail. He had done so without major damage to his aircraft or wounds to his body. Not so lucky were eight other pilots from the *Hancock*. They were either dead, captured or missing-in-action. Another six weeks and the ship would commence its homeward journey to the West Coast of the United States.

Mike checked his TACAN indicator which registered 25.8 miles to the Danang Air Station. "Home Plate, Diamond eight-seven is switching to Danang Approach. Thanks for watching me."

Mike flipped through the approach plates on his knee pad. Finding the plate for Danang, he placed it on top where he could refer to it during his approach and landing.

"Danang Approach Control, Diamond eight-seven is an Alfa-Four Charlie at twenty-five miles out for landing. Low fuel state."

"Roger, Diamond eight-seven, you are cleared for landing upon arrival. Altimeter is 28.99. Recommend you maintain five thousand feet of altitude until final approach. We've had reports of snipers firing small arms at landing aircraft."

CHAPTER 22

Mike Murphy enjoyed the long hot shower in Danang's BOQ. Aboard ship, where fresh water was always at a premium, crew members were restricted to a few seconds of water to wet the body, turning the water off and soaping the body, then a few more seconds of water to rinse off the soap. Mike toweled himself thoroughly then returned to the small room with four cots. The bachelor officers' quarters at Danang consisted of a large wooden building with a tent-like canvas top. It was internally divided into small cubicles with partitions and metal lockers.

Mike dressed in new underwear and fatigues he had purchased at the base exchange after leaving his wounded A-4C Skyhawk with the Marine Corps maintenance detachment for repairs. It would be the next morning before the Skyhawk would be ready to fly back to the USS *Hancock* in the Gulf of Tonkin. Mike slipped his feet, adorned with new khaki socks, into the scuffed pair of flight boots he had worn since reporting for active duty over a year ago.

A Marine Corps captain that was sharing the BOQ room with Mike directed him to the officers' bar. It had been nearly two months since the *Hancock* was in Hong Kong for five days of rest and recreation, and that was the last time that Mike had tasted liquor.

"A double gin martini with three olives," Mike told the bartender. Mike lit a cigarette and inhaled deeply. Sweeping the room with his eyes, Mike detected a goodly number of females, probably military nurses and a few war correspondents. These marine and air force fly-boys really have it made compared with their navy counterparts aboard carriers. Long, hot showers, booze and women. What a way to fight a war. Much better than being on a big iron ship that rolled and tossed and pitched twenty-four hours a day, where booze and women were not allowed, and the runway was only several hundred feet in length.

The bartender placed the double martini on the bar in front of Mike. "Fifty cents," he said.

"Fifty cents? What is this...some kinda rot-gut gin?"

"No, sir. Beefeaters. We have Tanqueray, if you prefer."

"No. Beefeater's fine. Thank you." Mike took a double swallow ...paused for a moment, then took another double gulp which caused him to choke. "Damn!...that's good stuff."

There was loud laughter at the other end of the bar, and Mike observed a group of men, some in flight suits and other in fatigues, gathered around a shorter individual in civilian clothing. Another loud laugh from the group, but this time it struck a familiar chord—a laugh Mike had heard before. Mike leaned forward over the bar to get a better look at the group but recognized no one he knew. Maybe someone he had met or known at A-4C refresher training at Leemore —there had been a number of Marine Corps' pilots in the program with him. The bartender delivered another round of drinks to the rowdy group, and the man in civilian clothing turned to pay the tab. With long stringy hair and a three or four day beard, he certainly wasn't a military officer. Mike caught a full view of the man in the mirror behind the bartender. He wore a faded yellow T-shirt with the letters KCRP across the chest in bold blue letters. "Jesus Christ!" Mike shouted. "Buzz Bigsby." Mike raised his hand high above his head. "Hey, Buzz."

The man leaned across the bar and looked toward Mike. "I'll be goddamned...Mike Murphy." He pushed his way through the circle of men surrounding him and made his way toward Mike. "What the hell are you doing here?"

"What the hell am I doing here? I belong here. What the hell are you doing in this part of the world? Bigsby Air Services flying supplies into Nam now?" Mike shook hands with the ex-discjockey turned pilot.

"Bartender," shouted Buzz over the roar of the revelers, "bring my old buddy a double martini." Turning to Mike, "Beefeaters, isn't it?"

Mike nodded.

"Beefeaters," Buzz shouted even louder, "and a double of whatever I'm drinking." Buzz nodded toward a table at the rear of the club, and Mike followed him toward it.

"Christ, Mike. I never thought I'd see you over here. Thought you were flying off carriers."

"I am, Buzz. The *Hancock*, out in the gulf. I had to land at Danang this afternoon because my tailhook wouldn't come down. I took some flak in the tail that jammed the hook. The marines are working on it now. It'll be ready in the morning and I'll fly it back out to the ship."

An attractive young Vietnamese lady brought their drinks to the table. Mike reached for his wallet.

"No way, Mike," Buzz said. "I'll get these. I owe you...besides, I make a lot more money than you."

"Jesus, Buzz, I can't believe you're out here. What's doing with your air service?"

"Down the drain. Right after you left to go back in the navy, we started losing money. Doris pulled the plug. She offered me a non-flying job with Air Arizona...a gopher job. I didn't want any of that shit. I answered an ad in the *Arizona Republic*: Pilots wanted. Apply in person at the Marana Air Park."

"An airline job, Buzz?"

"Yeah...sort of. The spook airline!"

"Never heard of 'em. Spook Airline?"

"Air America, Mike. We call it the spook airline because of what we do. Hell, we've flown opium, bombs, ammo, dropped spies in China, special units into North Vietnam. We fly so low most of the time that we have to dodge our way through the tree tops. Our slogan is *anything, anywhere, any time...professionally*."

"Yeah, Buzz, I've heard of Air America. Run by the CIA, isn't it?"

"So I hear. My paychecks come from an outfit called Pacific...in Delaware. I don't ask questions. They promised me a thousand bucks a week and a box to come home in. So far they've lived up to their part of the deal."

"What are you flying, Buzz? The only Air America planes I've seen are C-47 Gooney Birds."

"Christ, Mike...we have a little of everything—Boeing 727's, C-46's and -7's, C-123's, Otters, Cessnas, PC-6's, and helicopters. I fly mostly into Laos, so I fly the Cessnas and PC-6's. The PC-6 is called the Pilatus Porter. It's a high-wing monoplane with an enormous turbo-prop engine. I—"

"Laos? We're not fighting in Laos...are we, Buzz?"

"Well, someone sure the hell is. I get shot at damn near every time I fly into there. Laos has three kinds of weather: foggy, windy, rainy. The flying over Northern Arizona was sure good training for me."

"Damn! I thought flying over North Vietnam was tough. I can't believe you're flying into Laos."

"You go down in North Vietnam, Mike...you're a P.O.W. If I go down in Laos, I'm S.O.L.—shit outa luck!"

"What are you doing in Danang, Buzz? You don't operate outa here, do you?"

"Naw. Mostly out of Tan Son Nhut and Bien Hoa. I had a few days free, so I jumped on one of our Gooney Birds headed this way. I run a little business on the side, Mike."

"Business?" Mike caught the attention of the cocktail waitress. "Another round here, please."

"I pick up skin flicks...you know, porno movies, in Hong Kong and the Philippines. They only cost a few bucks there. I sell them in-country for fifty...sometimes seventy-five bucks. It's not legal, but almost everyone over here has a little business on the side. You should see some of the illegal crap I haul for some of the big-wigs out here."

The cocktail waitress delivered their drinks. Buzz paid again, leaving a sizable tip.

"How much longer you have out here, Mike?"

"Another six weeks...then we'll head home through Yokosuka and Pearl Harbor. I'll probably get another deployment out here in about eighteen months...if the war's still on."

"Shit, Mike, this war will be on forever. Too goddamned much money being made out here to ever end it. You plan on staying in the navy, Mike?"

"I do, Buzz. I'm regular navy now...not a reserve. Doris can run her friggin' airline anyway she wants." Mike took a long drink of his martini. "How're they doing when you left?"

"Great. They've got a whole fleet of F-27's. Tad's changed a lot. No more coveralls. Wears a coat and tie most of the time. Big shot. Doris is her same old self...wheeling and dealing. They even have some DC-8's running soldiers to and from Nam."

"No thanks. I'd rather be out here where I know who my enemies are." Mike finished his drink. "Buzz, I guess I had better get back to my room and get some shut-eye. I'll fly out to the ship early in the morning. They'll probably have me scheduled for a mission in the afternoon. It's been great talking with you. Maybe I'll—"

"Wait a minute, Mike. I'll go back with you. I'm outa here early in the morning also. I've just got to stop by the enlisted barracks for a few minutes and deliver some films." Buzz picked up the brown leather flight bag he had placed beside his feet.

Buzz threaded the government-issue 16 mm movie projector. "Sorry, Mike. The guys want to see one or two before they pay. They're short...fifteen minutes or so." Buzz turned on the projector. "Someone get the lights."

Mike eased into a chair behind the dozen or so enlisted men, mostly marines. The movie flickered to life on a white sheet the men had hung on the wall. A slim dark man with a huge black mustache, either an Italian or Mexican, peered through a window at two women who were undressing—neither particularly attractive. One, a brunette, was a bit more than pudgy, bordering on obese. The other, a red head, was overly lean with bones protruding here and there, and breasts that barely protruded at all. When fully undressed, they laid together on an un-made bed and began examining each other...poking and prodding. Just then, Senor Mustachio, who had been leering through the window, jumped through the open door, his mustache askew. The women tried to appear surprised—but it was obviously the third or fourth re-take, and the director apparently had given up on the scene. The man shed his clothing, except for his black socks, and leaped into the bed between the two *nymphs*.

"This is shit!" one of the onlookers shouted.

"Yeah," another added. "You brought this same movie last time and no one bought it."

"Okay...just a minute. Let me rewind it." Buzz stopped the projector and set it for rewind. "I've got a real hot one here I know you'll like."

Mike stood and stretched. "Buzz, I'm headed for the sack. Maybe I'll see you in the morning before I leave."

"Wait just a minute, Mike. This one's real good. I'll show it and we`ll get outa here."

Mike sat back down to accommodate his friend, but he really didn't want to see another skin flick. He rocked his chair back against the wall and closed his eyes. He heard the projector start again as he dozed off.

Moments later he heard: "Wow!" "This is more like it." "Look at those two gals...they're gorgeous." "Gee, what a pair of knockers." Mike opened his eyes. On the sheet before him in spectacular living color, Dolores DeLabia and Bobbi Bleaugood clung to the legs of Arturo Casanova as he slowly dragged them across the deck toward the cabin of the yacht.

"Holy shit!" Mike cried out, but his voice was lost in the cat-calls and whistles of the men watching the movie.

"Jeez, that dude's really hung. Wonder where they got him?"

"Hey, look what that blonde's doing. She's got his...holy cow!"

"I wonder where they get people to make movies like this? I'd sure volunteer." The room filled with laughter.

"Hey, Buzz, this is more like it. I'll take a copy."

"Me too. Got any more movies with these same actors?"

Mike Murphy slipped quietly out the rear door of the barracks into the muggy night air. In the distance he could hear the chatter of automatic rifle fire and the occasional boom of a canon or mortar. Far off to the east he could see parachute flares descending from invisible aircraft.

AIR ARIZONA

CHAPTER 23

The squawk box in ready room three crackled, "Pilots, man your aircraft."

Lieutenant Commander Mike Murphy and Lieutenant Johnny Watson, girded for battle in olive-green flight suits, torso harnesses, survival kits, *May Wests* and .38 caliber revolvers tucked in shoulder holsters, lumbered their way toward the escalator that would take them to the flight deck of the USS *Hancock*.

The mission required only two A-4C Skyhawks from VA-216, two F-8U Crusaders from VF-24 and one E-1B Tracer from VAW-11. The two Skyhawks would bomb the only two remaining pumping stations in North Vietnam capable of transferring petroleum from ships to tanks ashore. The Crusaders would provide fighter cover overhead in the event the Skyhawks were jumped by enemy fighter aircraft. The Tracer, known affectionately by the Air Group as *Willy Fudd*, would fly high over the carrier to provide radar tracking and guidance to mission aircraft and early warning surveillance for ships in the task group. It was a mission that had been attempted before without success, and two of the four aircraft involved had been downed by surface-to-air missiles. No parachutes were observed and both pilots were declared missing-in-action. The other two aircraft had suffered moderate damage from anti-aircraft flak and were unable to make runs on the target.

The two Skyhawk pilots reached the top of the escalator and

stepped out into brilliant sunlight that bathed the flight deck of the *Hancock*. Lieutenant Watson signaled a thumbs-up to Mike. "Good luck, commander. Let's knock the crap outa them this time"

Mike responded with a similar thumbs-up. "Roger that, Johnny. Buy you a cup of coffee when we get back." Mike's comment was hollow. He was apprehensive and had an uneasy feeling about the mission. North Vietnamese SAM sites and anti-aircraft batteries proliferated the area around the fuel farm. He glanced at the watch on his wrist. It was 0733, twenty-seven minutes to launch. The date was July 7, 1966.

Mike located his aircraft, Diamond 92, just aft of the port catapult. It was a good aircraft that he had flown many times. He was at least happy with his aircraft assignment. Aircraft, even of the same model, had their individual quirks and differences. Some were a little heavier on the controls or a little slower to respond, some required radical trim settings to overcome repairs to battle damage, and others simply did not feel right without explanation or reason.

Mike quickly completed his pre-flight inspection of the Skyhawk, checking the jet intakes for foreign objects, the nose wheel and strut, access doors, static vents, antennas. Rubbing his hand along the leading edge of the wing, he checked for dents and wrinkles. Under the wing he checked the security of the bombs attached to wing stations and at the rear of the aircraft, the flight control surfaces, jet exhaust and tailhook. Satisfied that all was in order, he climbed the ladder into the cockpit.

The enlisted plane captain assisted Mike in attaching his parachute and restraining straps. "Going hunting this morning, commander?" the plane captain asked.

"Right, Grogan." Mike took his helmet and kneeboard the plane captain had been holding for him. "Going after big game today. Up north. This bird ready to fly?"

"Yes, sir. Been over her with a fine-toothed comb. She'll get you there and back. Just don't let any of those little slant-eyed bastards put any holes in her."

Mike nodded with a smile as he put on the helmet with its attached oxygen mask. He began checking the position of all switches in the cockpit and proceeded with the *pre-start* checklist.

The plane captain climbed down and removed the ladder from the aircraft.

The flight deck bullhorn screamed, "Check all loose gear on deck. Stand clear of all propellers, rotors and jet exhausts. Standby to start the helo."

A second later, "Start the helo. Standby to start the prop and jets."

Mike completed the check list and awaited the command to start jets.

"Launch the helo," commanded the flight deck bullhorn. Mike knew that somewhere on the after flight deck the H-2 Seasprite from HC-1 was lifting to provide plane guard protection for the launching aircraft. Should an aircraft crash into the sea after launch, the helicopter would attempt to rescue the downed pilot. Trained swimmers onboard the helo could jump into the water and assist the pilot into a sling which would lift him to safety.

"Start the prop and jets."

Mike observed a thumbs-up signal from his plane captain indicating all clear for engine start. He engaged the Crank Switch and moved the throttle to Start. The Tailpipe Temperature Gauge indicated a rising temperature and Mike adjusted the throttle to 10 percent rpm. He checked for oil pressure, and observing a rise, he signaled the plane captain to disconnect the external power cable. He had a clean start. Quickly he worked through the *post start* checklist.

The flight deck became suddenly alive with screaming banshees. The Willy Fudd was already being positioned on the starboard catapult for launch, its two Wright R-1800 reciprocating engines popping and snapping as it crept forward to the catapult shuttle. Much slower than the jets, the Willy Fudd would be launched first to begin its labored climb to 15,000 feet.

Mike, as flight leader of the attack aircraft, would be shot off the port catapult followed by the other Skyhawk off the starboard cat. The Crusaders would be launched with afterburners on and wings in the high incident position to facilitate lift-off of the heavy fighter aircraft.

A yellow-shirted flight deck director caught Mike's attention with his right hand held high over his head indicating he was now directing the aircraft. Another signal by the director to plane handlers on each side of the aircraft commanded the wheel chocks to be removed. On the director's signal to taxi forward, Mike released the brakes and added throttle. The A-4C inched forward.

Another director beside the port catapult took over and signaled for a nose steering bar to be attached to the nose wheel of the aircraft. The nose of the Skyhawk bounced up and over the catapult shuttle. Another signal brought the aircraft to a halt.

"Diamond niner-two, Pri-Fly. How do you read?"

Mike keyed his radio switch on his throttle. "Diamond niner-two reads Pri-Fly loud and clear."

Mike felt the aircraft lurch forward as the catapult put tension on the Skyhawk. A cable attached to the aircraft and the shuttle would provide the connection that would slam the twenty-seven thousand pound airplane from a standstill to 135 knots of airspeed in two and a half seconds. Mike busied himself with the *before takeoff* checklist.

"Launch aircraft," came the command over Pri-Fly frequency.

The Willy Fudd squatted as its engines came to full power. A signal from the catapult officer sent the E-1B Tracer down the starboard cat and into the air.

The catapult officer moved to the port cat. With his right hand extended over his head, index finger extended, he rotated the hand rapidly in a circle. Mike took the throttle to full power. The Skyhawk danced, ready to go.

Mike made one final check of his engine and flight instruments. Satisfied all was ready for launch, he hooked his index finger in the throttle grip to prevent his hand and throttle from moving aft during the tremendous surge forward when the steam catapult fired. He saluted the catapult officer with his right hand and quickly returned it to the control stick. "Let's get this great fuckin' adventure in the air," he shouted to himself. He held his head erect and pushed it hard against the head rest. The cat officer swung his right hand over his head and knelt to the deck, pointing toward the bow of the ship. A breath later, the catapult fired.

Mike and his A-4C Skyhawk shot forward. The bow end of the carrier raced by and Mike was over blue water. He raised the landing gear and eased the nose skyward into a climb. Changing radio frequency, he called, "Home Plate, Diamond niner-two airborne. All systems go."

"Roger, niner-two. When playmate joins, switch to channel six for control."

Moments later, Diamond eight-one, piloted by Johnny Watson, joined on Mike's right wing. A call to the Willy Fudd provided them a vector to the target near Hiaphong. The speedier Crusaders, launched after the Skyhawks, were already climbing above them to take their combat air patrol positions.

Time to rest a few moments before the action starts. Mike fished a cigarette from his flight suit pocket and lit up. He had only time for a few deep drags before reaching the area where surface-to-air missiles could reach them. He extinguished the cigarette and cinched up his lap and shoulder harness.

A number of short vectors were given to the Skyhawks by the Willy Fudd controllers to prevent enemy radar operators from discerning their intended target. As they crossed over the coastline, the air controller recommended dropping to low altitude.

"Okay, Johnny, let's hit the deck," Mike broadcast over tactical frequency. He pushed the Skyhawk's nose downward.

"Diamond-leader, Willy. Your final heading to target is 025 degrees."

"Roger, Willy. Heading 025." Mike banked sharply right to pick up the target heading. The Skyhawks approached red line speed as they leveled fifty feet above the terrain.

"Diamond-leader, Willy. You're at I.P. now."

Mike glanced quickly to his kneepad where a map of the target area was clipped. He confirmed their position at the initial point for attack. He realigned his heading to account for the surface winds and armed his ordnance panel for a two-bomb drop. He could see the pumping stations ahead. As briefed, he would take the station to the east and his wingman the station to the west. They would each drop two bombs on their first pass and, if necessary, two more on a second pass.

Red streaks shot by Mike's Skyhawk. The anti-aircraft batteries had locked on them. Mike pushed the nose down again bringing the aircraft within a few feet of the ground. He had to ease up and over the wire security fence around the pumping stations. He could see trucks on the ground and people dashing for cover. He pickled the bomb switch and two five-hundred pound bombs, one from each wing, plummeted earthward. He jerked the control stick back into his lap and the A-4C shot skyward.

"Diamond-lead, Checkertail four-seven," called a Crusader from high above the target area. "You have a miss at twelve o'clock."

Mike rogered the transmission and banked sharply left to see the target. Black smoke billowed from a warehouse just north of the pumping station. "Damnit!" Mike said aloud.

"Diamond-two, Checkertail four-seven, you have a bullseye."

Mike could see flames erupting from the western station.

"Diamond-two, this is Diamond-lead. I'm going around for another run. Buster outa here and I'll join you over the water."

"Jesus, Mike! Don't go in there again. The flak's so thick you can walk on it. Let's both get the hell outa here."

"Negative, Johnny. One more run on the east station. I'll join you later."

Mike put the Skyhawk in a diving left turn and re-armed the panel for two more bombs. The sky filled with red hot metal. The A-4C buffeted wildly as it collided with shards of shrapnel. He leveled the wings and bore directly toward the pumping station. A red *Fire*

Warning light illuminated in the cockpit. Mike ignored the warning as he put the station in the center of his sight. Steady. Steady. Now! Mike released the two five-hundred pounders and banked steeply in a right turn that would take him out over the harbor.

"Bullseye, Diamond-lead. Bullseye," called one of the Crusaders overhead. "Better get your ass outa there. All hell's breaking loose."

Mike zoomed by several ships in the harbor at deck level. Machine guns from the boats ripped open the Skyhawk like a can opener. Mike pulled back hard on the stick to gain altitude. The aircraft canopy shattered. Blood filled his eyes and oxygen mask. He ripped off the mask and wiped the blood from his eyes with the sleeve of his flight suit, but he still couldn't see.

"Diamond-lead, get out...the whole damn plane is in flames. Eject! Eject!"

Mike tried to reply but couldn't. His right arm and hand were numb. He tried to reach overhead for his seat ejection handle, but it was impossible. Any minute, he thought, he would crash into the ground or water. It would all be over. He could feel the hot breath of fire that engulfed him. Another try for the ejection handle. He pulled. His body shot upward and was hit by a sledge hammer of rushing air. His legs numbed. He was tumbling in space. He still could not see except for the red ooze that filled his eyes. With his left hand he lifted his right arm and coaxed it toward the parachute D-ring. Easing his right fingers around the ring he broke it free from its elastic holding. Again with his left hand, he pushed his right arm across his body.

A sharp jerk snapped his arms downward. He was descending slowly beneath a parachute canopy. Descending to what? Water? Land? Buildings? Trees?

He hit hard. He was on ground. He ripped off his helmet and mask and wiped vigorously at his eyes. He could see...a little, but could not make out where he was. Voices. He heard voices...foreign voices. They were near him. He tried to stand but fell at each attempt. He pulled the .38 revolver from its holster. He tried again to stand. He couldn't. Pain shot down his right leg. Incredible pain. He reached down for the leg with his left hand. There was nothing there.

AIR ARIZONA

CHAPTER 24

The bus bounced to a stop at the Gia Lam Airport. It was the first in a convoy of buses and white ambulances marked with Red Cross pennants to arrive there on the twelfth day of February, 1973. Prisoners, dressed in blue-gray jackets, blue pants and shirts, and black shoes, filed off the bus and formed two lines of ten prisoners each. Michael Murphy hobbled into ranks using the new crutches provided by the Red Cross on his departure from the *Hanoi Hilton* POW camp. It replaced the crude wooden crutch he had used for the nearly seven years in the *Hanoi Hilton* to compensate for his right leg which had been amputated just above the knee.

A C-130 Hercules aircraft was parked across the field several hundred yards from where the prisoners stood in ranks. Two other buses had also disembarked prisoners, and they too stood in similar lines. A large aircraft which Mike could not identify had just landed and was taxiing toward the ranks of prisoners. Someone in the line behind Mike called out, "It's a C-141." It was an aircraft Mike had never seen.

The guards marched the prisoners of war forward to a table where two senior officers sat—an American colonel and a North Vietnamese lieutenant colonel. Mike recognized the North Vietnamese officer as the one the prisoners called *Rabbit*.

Rabbit called out the names of the prisoners to come forward to the table, the injured and wounded first. "Commander Michael

Mitchell Murphy, United States Navy."

Mike moved forward to the table receiving a salute from the American officer.

"Welcome back, commander. You're on your way home."

An air force sergeant took Mike's arm and assisted him toward the C-141. As they reached the lowered rear ramp of the aircraft, a lovely blonde flight nurse in a form fitting flight suit took Mike's arm and helped him up the ramp. "What's your name," she asked.

"Michael Mitchell Murphy, Lieutenant Commander, United States Navy," he answered curtly, not sure that this whole thing wasn't another North Vietnamese ploy. So many times before they had been promised release, but it never came. This was like a dream. Maybe it was.

"Well, Mike Murphy," the flight nurse said as she placed a gentle kiss on his cheek. "Welcome back. My name is Valerie Morris. Please call me Val."

Tears came to Mike's eyes, his throat tightened, his voice cracked. "Thank you...Miss...Val." The tears flowed freely down his cheeks.

Valerie Morris helped Mike to a seat. She buckled the seat belt gently around his mid-section. "Save this seat," she said, pointing to a seat beside Mike. "I'll be back in a few minutes."

A total of forty ex-prisoners of war were assisted into the cavernous fuselage of the C-141. The crew raised the ramp and buttoned up the hatches. The engines whined into operation, and the large aircraft taxied into position for takeoff. Val seated herself next to Mike. With a smile she said, "Let's get this show on the road. I bet you're anxious to get home, aren't you Mike?"

The engines roared to a crescendo and the big plane lurched forward. Under his breath Mike said, "Yeah. Let's get this great fu...ah...adventure in the air.

"What was that, Mike?" Val asked.

"Nothing. Sorry. I was thinking about something else...a long time ago." Mike closed his eyes.

As the C-141 lifted into the air there were shouts and cheers from the repatriated prisoners. "Sonofabitch! We made it." "Yahoo!" "We're outa here."

Val took Mike's right hand into hers and squeezed. A hint of a smile crossed Mike's face. He finally believed.

Enroute to Clark Air Force Base in the Philippines Mike learned from Val that 116 POW's had been released this day, forty on each of two C-141's and 36 on the C-130, which also carried a medical team of doctors and nurses. A civilian doctor from the state department onboard Mike's flight quizzed the ex-prisoners to determine the names of other prisoners that they knew were in captivity. Additionally, he told them that when they landed in the Philippines there, would be a red carpet, a lot of military brass, TV cameras and correspondents, and probably thousands of well-wishers.

As they crossed over the Gulf of Tonkin, the USS *Enterprise* radioed a welcome home message.

The senior officer among the prisoners announced that he would exit the aircraft first and say a few words. After that, the others would exit in order of shoot-down. That meant several others would exit before Mike. He was glad he would not be one of the first few.

The flight to Clark Air Force Base took four hours during which time there was a lot of shouting and yelling, handshakes and back-pats, crying and praying.

Valerie Morris told Mike that she was from Santa Fe, New Mexico, and that she had attended the University of New Mexico. She entered the air force as a flight nurse four years ago and would soon be released from active duty. "I plan to return to Albuquerque," she said, "and resume my nursing career in a federal government program which provides health care to Indians living on reservations. That's why I went into nursing in the first place. I have always felt close and at home with the Indian people."

Mike started to relate his experience delivering an Indian baby in a Cessna 180 over Payson, Arizona, but was interrupted by a loud cheer that broke out in the cabin. They had just crossed the coastline of the

Philippine Island of Luzon, and the C-141 started to descend.

A short time later the landing gear of the large aircraft dropped to the down position followed by the extension of the wing flaps. The plane shuddered as it slowed to approach speed. Touchdown was greeted with a thunderous roar from the passengers.

The aircraft taxied quickly to the ramp area where it came to a halt. There was confusion as the men stood up and tried to arrange themselves in the order they would exit the aircraft. Valerie assisted Mike into his place in line. She gave his hand a final hard squeeze. "I'll try to visit you later in the hospital if they'll let me." She handed Mike a slip of paper. "In case I miss you at the hospital, here's my phone number and address in the states. Please call."

The line moved forward a few feet then stopped. Mike could hear a loudspeaker outside the aircraft blaring out words, but he couldn't understand them. Again the line moved forward. In a few minutes he reached the exit door and stepped out on to a low ramp. He was startled by the thousands of men, women and children that had massed for their arrival. Many were in uniform but some wore civilian clothing. At the bottom of the steps down from the ramp there was a long red carpet where a navy admiral stood welcoming each man.

Mike moved forward and positioned his crutches to negotiate the first step. A crewman from the C-141 grabbed Mike's right arm. "Can I help you, sir?"

"No. Thank you. I'm gonna do this all by myself." He placed a crutch leg on the first step and shifted his weight to it as he swung his left leg down to the step. Seven years of maneuvering on one leg had developed the muscle in his left leg and in his arms, and his confidence to move about unaided. He repeated the procedure again for the next step and the remaining steps to the carpet. Finally he placed his left foot and crutches on the red carpet. Putting his full weight on his left leg he snapped his right arm to his forehead saluting the admiral. "Lieutenant Commander Michael M. Murphy, United States Navy, returning for duty, sir."

The admiral returned the salute. "Welcome home, commander."

The television cameras moved in as close as the security ropes and guards would allow. The crowd cheered and whistled their greetings to the one-legged navy pilot as he made his way to the waiting bus. Signs held high above the crowd read: WE LOVE YOU. WELCOME HOME. GOD BLESS YOU.

Several more men boarded the bus after Mike. The doors closed and the bus drove slowly off toward the base hospital. All along their route there were people waving, cheering, throwing kisses.

At the hospital they were led along freshly scrubbed white walls to rooms with six beds, each enclosed by a curtain. Mike did not recognize the other five men who came into the room, but it didn't matter. They all shook hands and hugged, each saying his name, his service and the date he was shot down.

What a change from the pigsty he had spent almost seven long years in; no foul odor of human feces; no sharp pungent smell of rotting food he had eaten to survive; no prodding bayonets from sadistic guards. Any minute, Mike thought, he would awaken to find it all a dream. He had had other such dreams before waking to reality.

"Showers everyone." A nurse in a crisp white uniform stuck her head in the door to their cubicle. "Soap and shampoo are on your beds."

Mike undressed and slipped on the blue robe that was on his bed. He took the shampoo and soap, and aided by his crutches made his way to the shower room. Others were already in the shower laughing and teasing like high school football players after a hard-fought and meaningful victory. Mike slipped off the robe placing it on a hook outside the shower. A hush fell over the shower room as Mike entered. The stump of his right leg was not pretty. The crude amputation by the North Vietnamese doctor had left a bulging mass where his knee should be.

Mike smiled. "The hot water looks great. I can hardly wait to get in."

The laughter and horseplay resumed. Mike stood under the flood of hot water a full fifteen minutes, then spent another ten minutes shampooing his hair several times.

"Chow," someone outside the shower yelled.

Mike toweled himself dry, put on his robe and made his way back to the room. On his bed were clean hospital pajamas and a large safety pin. Mike pulled on the pajamas. He rolled the right leg to the stump and secured it with the pin.

At the entry to the mess hall, a team of doctors questioned each ex-prisoner as they entered. "Any major problems? Injuries? Can you move everything?"

The man in front of Mike mentioned to the doctors that he had had worms in his stool and severe cramping. A doctor handed him a large card stamped *BLAND DIET*. Although Mike had suffered from the same symptoms, he decided not to mention it. He had been on a bland diet for almost seven years.

The team of doctors asked Mike the same questions and registered embarrassment when Mike slapped the rolled pajama pants leg.

Mike filled his tray with steak, eggs, french fries and two large chocolate milk shakes. Finishing this, he returned to the line and concocted a massive hot fudge sundae. When he could swallow no more of the gooey ice cream, he left the mess hall and returned to his room.

Mike was shocked to find a party in progress. One of his room mates was pouring Jim Beam whiskey from a large bottle into paper cups. "Where'd that come from?" Mike asked.

"Damned if I know," was the answer. "It was here when we returned from chow. Next room over has Johnny Walker scotch. Across the hall they have Beefeaters gin. Want a glass, Mike?"

"No thanks, guys. It's not your company I'm leaving, but I'm going across the hall and drown myself in Beefeaters."

The next day each of the men was measured for new uniforms and each had a debriefing session with an Intelligence Officer. Those requiring dental work were escorted to the dental clinic. Those requiring crowns had a temporary one installed and were told that permanent crowns would be done when they reached the states. Mike had one temporary crown installed on a front tooth that was broken in half when he bit down on a rock in his food at the *Hanoi Hilton*. Fortunately the absence of sugar in his prison diet prevented cavities from forming.

An orthopedic surgeon examined Mike's right leg. "Commander, you'll be returning to the Oak Knoll Naval Hospital for a prosthesis. You'll be amazed at how good they are now. You won't win any foot races, but you'll get around with little or no limp."

A navy captain that Mike did not recognize came by his room and handed him the silver oak leaves of a full commander. "Congratulations, Commander Murphy. You were promoted to full commander while you were in captivity. You should have a sizable amount of back pay coming."

The men were allowed to make phone calls home, but Mike wasn't sure who he would call or what he would say. He would call Tad Little when he reached California.

Four days later, Commander Michael M. Murphy departed the Philippines on a C-141 Starlifter. He had hoped to see Val Morris before he left, but she never came to the hospital. The Starlifter landed at Hickam Air Force Base in Hawaii for refueling at 0200, and at 1100 Pacific Standard Time, landed at Travis Air Force Base near Sacramento. From here Mike and a number of other former POW's were transported to the Oak Knoll Naval Hospital in Oakland, California.

CHAPTER 25

"Commander," Nurse Crenshaw called, sticking her head in the door of Mike Murphy's hospital room. "You have some visitors downstairs. They're on their way up now. Feel up to seeing someone?"

"I guess." Mike pulled the sheet and blanket over to cover his missing right leg. "Who are they?"

"The receptionist didn't say their names. It's a man and a women...maybe your parents."

"Don't have any. Some old friends probably. People I used to work with." Mike had been in the Oak Knoll Naval Hospital for three weeks since arriving back in the States. So far no one had visited; no one had called.

Mike heard footsteps outside his room. They stopped near his door. He heard muffled voices. More footsteps. Tad Little entered the hospital room dressed in a dark blue suit with a red tie. He was heavier than Mike remembered, and his hair was gray and thin.

"Mike! Damn it's good to see you. How you doing?"

Mike signaled for Tad to come closer.

Tad eased closer to the bed. "Sorry I haven't been up sooner, Mike...we're so damned busy now. Can't hardly get a weekend off anymore."

"Tad," Mike whispered. "I didn't have amnesia."

"What, Mike? I couldn't hear you."

"I didn't have amnesia."

"Amnesia? You mean in the P.O.W. camp you didn't have amnesia?"

"Fuck no!" Mike said in a loud voice. "In Nevada. I didn't have amnesia when I parachuted into that whorehouse." Mike smiled.

"Goddamnit, Mike. You had me scared. I didn't know what to expect. We saw you on television when you got off the plane in the Philippines. You looked like shit." Tad took the right hand Mike offered. "Hey, Doris...he's okay. Come on in."

Doris Kissling came through the door. Tall. Slim. Dressed in a tailored gray suit, auburn hair swept up in a French twist. "Mike!" She came forward and kissed Mike on the cheek. "You're looking great. You were skin and bones when we saw you on television. I brought you some cigarettes, Camels...and a bottle of Beefeaters."

"Hide the gin in my closet, Doris. Crenshaw will take it away from me if she sees it. Keep the cigarettes. I gave that vice up about seven years ago. A guard gave me a North Vietnamese cigarette, and it damned near killed me."

Doris put the gin in an overnight bag in Mike's closet.

"Maybe she won't find it here." Doris returned to the bed and sat on the edge momentarily but sprang up. "Sorry, Mike."

"It's okay to sit there, Doris. There's nothing there to sit on."

Doris flushed. "I'm sorry. I—"

"Don't worry about it. Sit down. You too, Tad. I know I don't have a right leg. You know it. I've learned to accept it."

"Are they gonna be able to do anything with it?" Tad asked.

"Doc says it'll be good as new...but not real. I've already been fitted for it."

"How long will you be in here?" Doris eased herself down on the bed beside Mike.

"Long time, I'm afraid. At least three months for physical therapy after I have my leg."

"You know," Doris said, "you still have a job with us. You can serve on the board of directors."

AIR ARIZONA

"Thanks, Doris, I appreciate the offer, but I'm just not sure right now what I want. I'd like to stay in the navy. They'll let me...but I won't be able to fly anymore, and you know that's always been my main interest. What's happening with Air Arizona these days? Still bouncing around the western states?"

"I'll let Tad tell you."

"Well, Mike, we're no longer a little fill in here...fill in there airline. The name's been changed to All American Airlines, and we no longer use the silver and turquoise paint scheme. We have seventy-five new Boeing 737 jet airliners...and twelve more on order. We cover all the western and mid-western states. We have two 747's on lease and fly two round trips daily from Phoenix to Honolulu. If we can get some slot times at Kennedy, we'll start daily 757 flights to New York. We've got the options on four brand new 757's. We had four DC-8's that we hauled personnel to and from Vietnam, but we don't need them anymore. They're for sale now."

Mike let loose a low long whistle. "Jesus! You guys haven't been standing still while I was vacationing in Hanoi. I never realized the company would get so big."

"Mike," Tad continued, "month in and month out, we're the number one airlines in the nation with on-time departures and arrivals. Also passenger satisfaction. Our employees are all stockholders in the company. Each month a part of their salary is paid in stock shares. When people own the airline they work for, they work a whole hell of a lot harder."

"Mike," Doris said. "Your shares in the company, which have split many times, are worth several million dollars. You're a millionaire ...and then some."

"Great, Doris. You always said we would be...but I never really believed you. You do make things happen."

"You just didn't have faith in me, Mike. Don't you really want to come back and be a part of All American Airlines. A part of our dream?" Doris paused. "You can have any job you want...just name it."

"It was your dream, Doris. Not mine. All I wanted was a little fly-by-night air service. Remember? I always fought you on expansion. I would come back on one condition. I'd like to be one of your line pilots. Fly those new jets all over the country. I would come back for that."

"Mike, I wish there was some way you could. You know that."

"I know, Doris. I know. Just dreaming. I'm not exactly sure what I want to do just yet...but I have an idea. I spent a long time sitting in that stinking rat hole in North Vietnam. A long time to think...to wonder...to reason. How could a country as wise and strong and wealthy as ours get so fucked up. I wondered at first why no one came to get us, why no one seemed to care. We had the weapons, the man power, the know-how to end the war in days...not years. Buzz had the answer. The war in Southeast Asia wasn't about stopping the spread of communism. The war was to make money and build egos. It only stopped when the people, not the politicians, wised up and said *enough*. A lot of good lives were lost or ruined...on both sides. They were simply wasted. For what? There has to be a better way. For America and the world."

AIR ARIZONA

POSTSCRIPT

BUCK SKIN — promoted to director of maintenance, All American Airlines, 1973. He accepted the position with an elegant speech. No one knew, except Doris Kissling, that he had such a broad and intelligent vocabulary.

JUDY GEORGE — promoted to director of operations, All American Airlines, 1973. He won the Annual All Arizona Amateur Goat Roping Contest, 1980.

TIMOTHY LONGSHANK — choked to death on a piece of steak at a dinner honoring him for achievement in pornographic film, 1977. His final words as he lay gasping on the floor were, "Adventure! That's what I'm looking for. A great adventure." He had just started production on his latest film, *Here Come The Marines*. It was to be the first pornographic film with a cast of thousands.

ARTURO CASANOVA — died of complications from hepatitis in Hermosilla, Mexico, 1975.

PHILLIP LENS — won an Academy Award in 1978 for his nature film, *The Mating of Antelope*. He has produced and filmed numerous award winning documentaries. His next film, *The Death of a Black Widow's Mate*, is due for release soon.

DOLORES DELABIA — resumed the use of her given name, Dolores Mann, and was nominated for Best Supporting Actress, 1980. Although she did not win an Oscar, she has appeared in many highly acclaimed feature films.

AIR ARIZONA

BOBBI BLEAUGOOD — resumed the use of her given name, Roberta Bloom. She has appeared daily in one of America's favorite daytime soap operas since 1975.

BUZZ BIGSBY — reported missing in Laos after the crash of his Pilatus Porter aircraft, 1972. Unconfirmed reports say that he made his way to Thailand and now operates a bar and bordello in Bangkok.

COMMANDER COOL — retired to Sun City, Arizona, 1975. He is the proud grandfather of seven and great grandfather of eighteen. He enjoys teaching his great grandchildren how to fly radio controlled models in the desert north of Phoenix.

MICHAEL MURPHY LITTLEFEATHER — graduated from the Phoenix Indian School, 1975. He received a football scholarship to the University of Arizona and was a two-time All American linebacker. In 1980 he signed a multi-year contract with the Washington Redskins.

REGIS ROTHCHILD — served as presidential advisor to Richard Nixon. Convicted in 1974 of participation in the Watergate scandal, he served five years in a federal prison. He published his memoirs in 1981, and today frequently appears as a guest on various radio and television talk shows.

THADEUS AVERY LITTLE — married Doris Dushane Kissling, 1975. He is the president and CEO of All American Airlines.

MICHAEL MITCHELL MURPHY — elected to the Arizona State Senate, 1974. Four years later he successfully ran for the United States Congress. He served eight years in the House of Representatives, then made a successful bid for the United States Senate. Today he is a highly respected senator from the state of Arizona and serves on a number of important committees, including Armed Forces, Indian Affairs and Transportation. He chairs the Aviation Subcommittee. In 1975, he married Valerie Denise Morris, the flight nurse he met on the P.O.W. flight from the Gia Lam Airport.

When not in the nation's capital, they enjoy their home in Oak Creek Canyon, Arizona. He was overheard to say at the gavel opening the 1997 senate session, "Let's get this great fuckin' adventure in the air."

AIR ARIZONA

AIR ARIZONA — the off-the-wall, fly-by-night air charter service that started operation in 1957, with one dilapidated surplus twin-engine Beechcraft C-45, is now All American Airlines, a major United States air carrier operating a fleet of Boeing 737's, 747's and 757's to destinations throughout the continental United States, Hawaii, Alaska, Canada and Mexico.

AUTHOR'S AFTERTHOUGHT

From the very beginning this book had one intent: fun to write— fun to read. The first part has certainly been fulfilled. I hope the second part will be also. I fear I may have stepped on some toes with my lighthearted approach to some of the situations, and if so, I do apologize. One of my first readers said: "In one book you have managed to piss-off women, Native Americans, Hispanics, TV and radio traffic reporters, disc jockeys, cowboys, people from Montana, Congress, the Navy, the Marine Corps, the CIA, porno movie makers, air services and airlines."

The one area I considered sacred, however, was the release and return of our POWs from North Vietnam. In no way did I want to make light of that. I feel our nation owes a great debt to those who returned and to the many who didn't. As a career navy officer and pilot, I also flew in the Vietnam conflict, and not a day goes by that I don't reflect on how fortunate I am to be here, whole and in good health.

I owe a very special debt of gratitude to Everett Alverez, Jr. and Anthony Pitch, whose book, *CHAINED EAGLE* (Dell Publishing, New York, 1989), gave me a true insight into the events that occurred on February 12, 1973, and the weeks that followed.

Other Books Available Through The Compass Rose Publishing Group

The Lieutenant Who never Was
A novel by Tom Smith

The amazing story of a navy pilot who appeared out of nowhere and disappeared likewise. Who was he? Where did he come from? Where did he go? The navy doesn't know. These questions are answered as you trace the life of a young man whose only goal in life is to be a naval aviator...any way he can!

Trade Paperback - 327 pages $12.95

Wind Sock Press
P.O. Box 55346
Phoenix, AZ 85078-5346

Personal inscriptions upon request.

Add $3.00 for priority mail or $1.50 for special standard mail
Arizona residents add 8% sales tax

* *

Quest for Gold
Gene Botts

A story of lost gold, forty-niners, and the Gold Rush days in California and Arizona. A possible solution to a hundred year mystery.

Trade Paperback - 195 pages $8.95

The Vulture
Gene Botts

The Vulture gold mine and old Vulture City are situated twelve miles and about a hundred years south of Wickenburg, Arizona. Conservative estimates place the value of the gold taken from the mine during its heyday at more than twenty million dollars, but if embezzlement, fraud, and theft are taken into account, the figure could be twice that amount. This is the Vulture's story. It's true, but reads like a novel.

The Border Game
Gene Botts

What the hell is going on? Why can't we enforce our immigration laws? Written by a 30 year veteran of the INS. The Border Game entertains while it argues for a reasonable and responsible immigration policy.

Trade Paperback · 357 pages $14.95

Quest Publishing Group
4035 West Joan De Arc
Phoenix, AZ 85029-1049

Personal inscriptions upon request.

Add $3.00 to complete order for shipping and handling.
Arizona residents add 8% sales tax
* *

Wind Sock Press and Quest Publishing Group are imprints of the
Compass Rose Publishing Group